THE AMERICAN COLLECTION 2: MASTERING THE ART OF LOVE

Dixie Lynn Dwyer

MENAGE EVERLASTING

Siren Publishing, Inc.
www.SirenPublishing.com

A SIREN PUBLISHING BOOK
IMPRINT: Ménage Everlasting

THE AMERICAN SOLDIER COLLECTION 2:
MASTERING THE ART OF LOVE
Copyright © 2013 by Dixie Lynn Dwyer

ISBN: 978-1-62740-282-8

First Printing: July 2013

Cover design by Les Byerley
All art and logo copyright © 2013 by Siren Publishing, Inc.

Printed in the U.S.A.

PUBLISHER
Siren Publishing, Inc.
www.SirenPublishing.com

DEDICATION

To my reading fans,
I truly enjoyed writing *Mastering the Art of Love.*
This story is about three amazing, hard-working people, who thought that life was just about running away from bad memories and their hurtful pasts, and instead found true love when they least expected it.

Like a gorgeous painting that catches your eye with its uniqueness and invisible pull, similar is the process of finding love. The delight and excitement of an attraction and desire, like the first strokes of a painter's brush, it eventually turns into a completed work, a fulfilling relationship and bond.

May you enjoy the story.
Hugs!
~Dixie~

THE AMERICAN SOLDIER COLLECTION 2: MASTERING THE ART OF LOVE

DIXIE LYNN DWYER
Copyright © 2013

Chapter 1

Mariana Sparketta, or "Sparks" as her delivery friends liked to call her, could feel the sweat dripping down her back. Despite the forty-degree temperature outside on the city streets of Houston, an absolute cold front for the end of January, Mariana pushed along on her skateboard in hopes of delivering the package on time. Being a courier in the city was a bit rough sometimes. She had to deal with traffic, pedestrians, delivery vehicles, obnoxious desk clerks, and asshole business big shots. She swore to herself that once she achieved her college degree and landed a job, making it big, or at least ran her own art gallery, she would be the same quiet, sweet person she really was. But times were tough. Adapting to life on her own in Houston, after her mama dying suddenly, Mariana learned to overcome. So what, that it was taking a little extra time to finish college? She would do it. She had to. There was no Prince Charming, no winning the lottery, and basically men sucked.

"Watch it, moron!" she yelled as she maneuvered around a guy getting out of a taxi who nearly plowed into her. Well, like she was thinking, she would still be the nice, respectful person her mama raised her to be, outside of working as a courier. She had to be tough, and she had to dress the part, too. On Friday and Saturday nights she worked her second job serving food and hors d'oeuvres at parties for the wealthy and prominent in the Houston business district. College cost big bucks, and she had another whole two semesters until she finished and landed her degree. But she still had most of her college loans to pay, that bank loan left behind by mama, along with rent for her one-bedroom shit hole, four blocks from campus. That was a stupid decision, and she should have paid the extra money somehow so she wouldn't worry about getting mugged or raped on her way home late at night.

Taking those self-defense courses better not come in handy. Or the illegal pepper spray she carried, she hoped, that remained in her purse.

She pumped her foot harder against the concrete as she jumped the sidewalk and headed straight for the open door to the building. The doorman, Stan, was holding it open. She waved and continued on, thinking that he was being nice. He knew that it was a Friday and she needed to get her deliveries finished.

His eyes widened, and it was too late when she realized that he was holding the door for someone else. The well-dressed businessman with the obnoxious expression on his face shot daggers at her as she rolled on by, skateboard and all, then skidded to a halt by the front desk.

"Hey, Lucille. How are you today?" she asked as she placed the box on top of the counter then handed over the slip of paper for Lucille to sign.

"Hey, Sparks. You nearly took out Walters," Lucille said as she signed the slip of paper.

She shrugged her shoulders. Dressed in a hooded sweatshirt, knit hat with her hair tucked under, sunglasses, and knee and elbow pads over her skinny jeans, she pulled off punk kid really well. Probably too well for a twenty-four-year-old college student with big boobs. The tight shirts underneath held them in snug. The plus from this job was a great body from all the exercise.

"I'm in a hurry and I don't have time to wait."

She took the slip of paper from Lucille, placed it in her backpack, and turned around prepared to take off again on her skateboard when she felt the shove to her shoulder.

"Hey, kid, who the hell do you think you are coming in to this establishment on a skateboard? You nearly knocked me down. What company do you work for? I'm going to call them up and get your little ass fired," he yelled at her.

"I'm not the regular kid who delivers here," Mariana began to say, keeping a smile to herself that this moron thought she was a boy. He was a good-looking guy, but his arrogance was so obvious, it instantly put her on guard. Her petite figure and present outfit camouflaged her body well. She decided to go with it.

"I need to get going. It won't happen again," she said in her pretend deep boy voice then dropped the skateboard and started to push off when the guy grabbed her sweatshirt and backpack and pulled her back. She fell to the ground, her shirt lifted, and it became quite apparent she wasn't a boy. She wanted the floor to swallow her up. She needed this job. How the hell was she going to get asshole to stop freaking out?

* * * *

"What seems to be the problem here, Walters?"

Jax Spaulding was standing in the lobby waiting for his brother Jameson to arrive for their meeting. He was fifteen minutes late. He hated to be late. Punctuality was the key to success. Standing in the corner, he watched as the young courier entered the building through the open door, nearly knocking Walters on his ass, which he would have loved to see, and then continued to the front desk as if nothing had transpired. He'd seen that kid before. Not just here in the business center but in other office buildings and locations throughout town. He sure did get around and really knew how to ride that skateboard. Jax was impressed.

As he approached the potential situation, Walters had grabbed the kid and made him fall down. Jax reached a hand down to the kid to help him up, and that was when he saw the belly ring. *Holy shit, he's a girl.*

"Take my hand, honey." As their hands touched Jax got a funny feeling in his stomach. It was almost like a spark of interest. He released her hand immediately, and she pulled down her sweatshirt.

"You didn't have a right to touch me. I can call the cops and charge you with assault, you know," she stated firmly to Walters.

"You won't do that, you're just a dumb kid on a skateboard. It's my word against yours. Get lost or I will call the police and get you fired," Walters said then walked away. The girl flipped him the bird behind his back, and a few people around them chuckled, including Lucille who worked behind the desk.

"Bye, Lucille," the girl said with a wave.

"Later, Sparks."

Jax didn't know why, but he grabbed her sleeve by her wrist. And what was with the name Sparks?

"Hey, wait a minute."

She jerked her arm away and then crossed her arms in front of her chest. He suddenly wished he could see her face, her eyes, or even her hair. She was camouflaged by the knit hat, sunglasses, and oversized hoodie. She was petite, too, and he liked petite women. But damn, did she look like a kid, a boy, in her getup. All he could do was focus on her lips that were definitely not lips a boy would have. She licked them at that moment and he felt fire in his belly. Jesus H. Christ, she'd better not be a boy and she'd better be over twenty-one. His body and his mind yelled, "Interesting."

"What's your real name?"

"Why, so you can get me fired?" Her fake deep voice was cheesy, but he figured she was playing up the boy thing still.

"I'm not going to get you fired. I wanted to know if you were okay. That fall was hard."

She stared at him. Or at least he assumed that she did behind those damn black sunglasses. *What color eyes does she have?*

"I'm fine and I've taken worse falls. Thanks for the help up but I need to go. I have one more delivery." She jumped on her skateboard and took off. Jax stared at her in shock as she skated through the lobby, across the marble flooring, and Stan held the door open for her with a smile on his face. Now suddenly her body didn't look so boyish. The hoodie covered her ass, but it was a woman's ass, not a boy's. He turned to look at Lucille who gave him a look as if wondering what was wrong with him.

"Lucille, who was that kid?"

She smiled. "She goes by the name Sparks, Mr. Spaulding. She's a woman, not a kid or a boy." His eyes widened despite the fact that his body had known immediately that he was a she. That little nudge of need formed in his belly. He really wished he could have gotten a look at her face, although her lips were very nice.

"What company does she work for?" he asked.

"It wasn't her fault, you know? Mr. Walters was nowhere near the door to exit. He makes Stan wait there and hold it for him, even if it means letting the bitter cold inside." Jax admired Lucille's loyalty to the delivery girl. He saw what Walters did. He was known to be an asshole and even in his own dealings with the man he found him obnoxious and frustrating.

"I know. I was just curious about her."

Lucille raised her eyebrows at him and he raised his eyebrows back at her.

His instincts had saved him too many times to remember as a Marine in the service. He wanted to know who this Sparks woman was. He had to see her face and to learn more about her. But by the way Lucille was watching him, he didn't want to come across as some kind of pervert. After all, he did verbally acknowledge the fact that he thought Sparks was a boy.

"Forget I asked. Hopefully she's okay from that fall."

"She's a tough one. Don't you worry."

But the odd thing was that he was worried, or perhaps that feeling was just plain curiosity.

Chapter 2

"Why are you so pissed off at me? I told you that I didn't want to meet these people, yet you said I would accompany you. I was late and that's it. You're lucky that I even showed up at all," Jameson said as he sat at the island in their studio apartment.

"This entire business was based on your ideas, your inventions. These people want us to run another program for them. We could be working on government-funded jobs shortly, too."

"I'm not interested in working for the government anymore. I've done my time serving in the military, I don't need to serve them more in civilian life, too. Stick to landing the private security accounts. Or better yet, buy that art gallery from Roldolpho. You've been eyeing it for the last two years. He's ready to sell, you can tell," Jameson responded with attitude.

Jax just couldn't figure his brother out. He remained in the service after his best friend, Sulter, was killed by insurgents and a year after Jax got out. Then he stayed another tour and finally just retired from the military eight months ago. Jax was trying to get him more involved with the business, but Jameson wasn't happy about it. They made a lot of money and their good friend Freda had introduced them to her investment broker, and now they were set for life. These were good times, and their private security business was growing and the alert device Jamison invested for special security detail was highly sought after. The deal they made landed them millions of dollars.

Maybe Jameson didn't want to continue. Perhaps his suggestion about buying the art gallery was right on. But Jax didn't have anything but the business and his brother Jameson. He was a coldhearted asshole most of the time. He didn't get close to people and especially women who seemed to always be after his money. Jax hated fakes and frauds. He didn't tolerate incompetence or laziness, and he was hard to please. He knew that but didn't give a shit.

"Believe me, I've been thinking about it. I'll think about it even more, tomorrow night when we attend the opening for that new artist, Belogio," Jax said as he poured himself a snifter of brandy. Their penthouse was huge, and the building contained all the amenities of high class and money. They also had a great view of the city skyline and a walk-out balcony for when they hosted a party. Of course they had only done that one time and hired a service to do everything. Thanks again to their good friend Freda.

She had quite the reputation as a business-savvy entrepreneur and widow. Her late husband Detrick Mulsberry was wealthy beyond sanity and owned everything from the boating and shipping industry to the art galleries and museums. She of course operated a small escort business, completely legit and nothing illegal. He had used her services in the past if he had an event to go to that required a date for social purposes and someone who had knowledge of the business world. Freda helped to arrange an escort for any businessmen in the city who needed a beautiful woman with brains to play the role at events. It was costly but well worth it. Freda only had one incident in the past where an escort wound up in trouble because her date decided that he wanted more than what the service offered. Freda called Jax and Jameson, and they immediately went to the young woman's aid and also took care of the jerk who tried to force her to have sex with him. Now, all Freda's escorts wore the special alert button. Jax and Jamison had each of the women followed and monitored on their dates.

"Oh, in regards to that little event, I don't think I feel like going tomorrow night," Jameson said.

"Oh come on, Jameson. I need you to come there. Freda's going and she was just asking about you last month when you didn't show to the Rothesburgh Gallery. There's going to be great food, too. I heard that Malone's is catering it."

That information seemed to perk Jameson up. He loved the food at Malone's.

"Fine, but I'm not staying the entire time, man."

* * * *

Mariana fixed her black skirt and adjusted her white blouse as best she could. Her breasts were big, and the tapered blouse was not exactly working here.

"Quit fidgeting, will ya? You look fucking gorgeous and especially with your hair pulled back like that. This is why Roldolpho always asks for you special. He adores you, Sparks," Tess, her coworker told her as she adjusted her French braid.

Roldolpho insisted that each server wear short, slim-fitting black skirts above the knee and white, button-down tapered blouses with the top few buttons undone. She tried to wear a camisole once and he reprimanded her for hiding her absolutely perfect body.

"Sparks?" *Speak of the devil.*

"Hello, Mr. Zenarack," she said to Roldolpho, and he shook his head and tsk-tsked at her.

"You did not just call me that?"

She chuckled and felt her cheeks warm. Roldolpho was totally charming, absolutely gorgeous, and gay. Tonight he wore a purple suit, but it wasn't like the Joker or some clown would wear. It was custom made just for him, and he wore it well. He had slicked back his black hair, his sleeves were rolled up revealing a light shimmering button-down shirt, and the cuffs were ironed stiff and held with gold-and-diamond cuff links. She hated to admit it, but he was a fine-looking man. He was in front of her pointing with his finger for her to twirl in a circle. That solid-gold pinky ring, with the single four-karat diamond, stood out like a beam of light. This was his routine. He checked everyone over, but especially her and Tess.

"Don't you think I didn't notice the two buttons? Now reach on in there and adjust those beauties of yours and undo another button. Men give tips to cleavage not because you served them a pig in a blanket," he stated then laughed to near hysteria. She shook her head and laughed then did as he told her. Poor Tess tried to do the same, but her breasts were not as full and perky as Mariana's.

"Now, you look hot. Listen, I have some important people coming tonight."

You have important people coming at all of these parties. God, I wish I had the nerve to ask him for a real job here. I know so much about artwork and running a gallery. It would be a dream come true to be fully involved in the business.

"I expect everything to go smoothly. Now, chop, chop!" he stated then clapped his hands, and the other servers were already heading toward the kitchen while she and Tess went to prepare to serve hors d'oeuvres.

* * * *

The gallery was jammed packed, but Jax and Jameson stood by Freda and Roldolpho as they spoke about the artist's work and the gallery itself.

Jax watched as Celia Armstrong attempted to seduce his brother by whispering in Jameson's ear and rubbing her palm against his chest. Jameson grabbed her wrist firmly yet gently.

"Take a walk. I'm not interested," Jameson nearly growled. Jax watched as the blonde wiggled her way over toward another group of men. Wealthy men Celia would love to trap. He locked gazes with Jameson, and Jameson glanced around the room as if totally bored and ready to bolt. That expression he used on Celia was priceless. Jameson was over six foot two, just like he was. With their muscular builds and that military attitude thrown in, they reeked of intimidation. But that also meant that they were chick magnets. Jax gave up hope of meeting someone nice and respectable. His brother hadn't shown any interest in any woman.

"This Belogio is not my cup of tea. Too much mishmash of colors and odd images," Roldolpho said.

"So what plans do you have for upcoming talent? Any unknowns?" Jax asked as Jameson sipped at a glass of champagne. His brother was uptight and had a bad attitude, but he was a good-looking guy. Jax was a man of action. He was demanding and expected a lot in return. When it came to women, he took extra precaution to not shit where he ate. He knew better. He felt that tightness in his chest as he tried to maintain a conversation with Roldolpho and Freda while thinking about his brother Jameson. They were close, and Jameson meant the world to Jax.

"Yes, I do have some new talent in mind. One of the artists has his work on display tonight," Roldolpho replied, and then Jax's attention went to the gorgeous brunette serving hors d'oeuvres. He hardly even focused on the platter of options. His gut clenched as their gazes locked. Her eyes widened as if she was surprised to see him or recognized him, and then she smiled as she moved the platter toward Roldolpho. He knew he had never seen her before. If he had, he would so be all over that. She looked sweet, almost virginal, despite her display of just the right amount of cleavage.

"Is that caviar?" Jameson asked, and the brunette looked at Jameson, and now Jax noticed his brother completely locked on the woman, too.

"Yes sir," she said then licked her lower lip. Jesus, her lips look familiar. *What the hell?*

She moved the platter toward Roldolpho and Freda, who smiled wide and took another sample. She nodded her head and began to walk away. Jax looked at Jameson, and Jameson was watching her, following her with his eyes as he held the caviar on a cracker in his hands. He and his brother hated caviar.

"So as I was saying, I do have a few new artists making their way onto the scene here in Houston. One of their paintings has been compared to Van Gogh," Roldolpho said then took a bite of the cracker with fish eggs on it.

"I never was a fan of Van Gogh," Jax said, uninterested in the conversation now. His eyes scanned the crowd, and he watched as men immediately took notice to the female server. One man in a tuxedo placed a bill in her hand and squeezed it over the money. He then leaned in next to her and whispered something. Jax was shocked at the possessive feeling that instantly came over him. He wondered what was wrong with him? She wasn't his. He didn't even know her, so why was he getting angry?

As he analyzed his feelings, he realized that he had lost sight of the beautiful young woman. She disappeared, and he felt the urge to look for her. Was he just horny? He had been in an odd state since yesterday and bumping into the skater girl. What was her name? Oh, yes, Sparks. He cleared his throat and tried to shake the odd thoughts from his head.

At that moment Roldolpho and Freda excused themselves, and Jax was left with Jameson.

"Hey, did you see that server? The brunette?" Jax asked his brother.

"Yeah, so what?"

"So what? You fucking locked on her like you used to lock onto a sniper shot target. She's beautiful."

"So go ask her out and do your thing."

"What's your problem, Jameson? You've been acting like a jerk lately and I've had enough." Jax walked away, fuming at his brother. He knew Jameson was interested in the brunette, and the fact that they both were in a state at her spoke volumes. He was going to find out who she was. Or he was going to hit someone. He was truly on edge here.

* * * *

Jameson was staring at a picture of God knew what. It was a mishmash of colors splattered across what was supposed to be a cityscape. He turned his head sideways and attempted to figure out what the scene was.

"Hors d'oeuvres, sir?" The sweet voice came from behind him, and he turned and locked gazes with large hazel eyes. The woman was much shorter than him, even in the slight heels she wore. Her hair was pulled back into a fancy style that showed off her slim, tan neck and perfect jaw. She had a petite nose and a gorgeous set of breasts on her. She was beautiful. She stared at him and then at the painting.

"I'm good. I wasn't too happy about the other stuff you brought over earlier."

"Oh, I'm so sorry, sir. Is there something specific that I can offer you? There are lots of hors d'oeuvres in the kitchen," she informed him as she held his gaze. Her cheeks looked flushed, and he wondered if she were feeling the same attraction that he was? He licked his lower lip, and she followed the movement. *Why am I thinking of a bunch of corny lines right now? You can offer me you on a platter.*

He cleared his mind and tried to remember how the hell to flirt with an attractive woman. She definitely wasn't like these other types. She looked sweet.

"I thought that Malone's was catering the event."

"They did, sir."

"Jameson?"

"The drink, sir?"

"No, the name is Jameson. You don't have to call me sir."

She stared at him as if he had two heads. "Okay."

He felt kind of stupid. It wasn't like he hadn't been with any women, and he just felt like an inexperienced teenager speaking with this woman. *What the heck.* He cleared his throat.

"I was hoping that Roldolpho had Malone's prepare those little shrimp quiche. Those are so good and the BBQ chicken strips on the stick."

She smiled, showing off bright white teeth.

"Wait right here, sir, and I'll see what I can do." She immediately walked away, and all he could do was watch her ass as she walked. It disturbed him that he wasn't the only one watching.

* * * *

Mariana swapped platters with Tess and headed back toward where the cute guy in need of a shave stood staring at a painting by Pazzarr. He looked so sad and just annoyed at being there. He was also next to that business guy who asked her name yesterday at the building. God, he was gorgeous and totally intimidating. By the way Roldolpho and a bunch of other snobby people were staring at him, the man must be important. She felt that instant attraction to not only him but this other guy, too. It was so crazy.

She grabbed the platter, placed a bunch of quiche and chicken strips on the stick on another platter. She covered it with a linen napkin to stay warm then headed out toward the guy. She didn't know why she was doing this. She didn't flirt and she wanted nothing to do with men, but he just looked so sad and sexy at the same time. If she could make him smile, then she was successful.

Mariana headed back toward the guy. He was still standing there and appeared annoyed.

"I wasn't sure you were coming back," he said to her, and he looked kind of intense.

"Of course, sir, I said I would. Here." She pulled the special cloth-covered plate out from under the main platter she held and handed it to him. He looked at the plate suspiciously and also at her in a guarded fashion. She leaned toward him. "I wouldn't poison you. I need this job. Enjoy, sir, oh, and don't try to figure out this painting. It's a new artist trying to mimic an old one. Pazzarr Rafique," she said then walked away. She looked over her shoulder just as he uncovered the platter. A smile formed across his face, and her heart soared. She wondered what the hell was wrong with her. She was acting like an idiot. He was probably loaded, too, just like the rest of the crew around here. She didn't need any bullshit.

Her old boyfriend Gavan, whom she dated through her first two years of college and who told her he loved her and wanted to marry her, turned out to be a lying, cheating shithead. He also was greedy for money, so when he cheated with some bimbo named Bambi, whose parents just happened to be filthy rich, he knocked her up and they got married. Money was definitely the root to all evil. But she needed money to pay her loans and her rent.

She took a deep breath then released it as she continued to make her rounds.

* * * *

"Did you or did you not see the instant attraction between the three of them?" Freda asked Roldolpho as they sat together on a couch that overlooked the gallery below.

"Are you kidding me? I nearly was shocked by the electric current. It was so unexpected."

"Tell me about the woman."

"Oh no, I know that tone of yours, Freda. You trying your hand at matchmaking now just because you run an escort service?" Roldolpho teased.

Freda smiled. There was something about that young woman that appealed to Freda. She wasn't sure what it was. From the seating above, Freda and Roldolpho both witnessed the interaction between the woman and Jameson. That poor, young man was filled with sadness, darkness, and pain. He was a handsome man and denied himself even the opportunity to explore a relationship. But the smile that the young woman brought to his face when she special delivered something Jameson liked was amazing to see. Freda was certain that she had never seen Jameson smile before. And Jax. Jax was all business and very assertive when it came to going after things he wanted. But he, too, stayed away from women aside from the one-night stands. She wasn't stupid. They were both afraid to open up their hearts and trust someone other than each other.

Roldolpho was snapping his fingers as a server approached. "Tell Tess to come up here."

The server nodded then hurried to a phone on the wall.

"You don't know anything about her?"

"I know that she's a hard worker. She works another job somewhere and is trying to achieve her bachelors degree."

"In what?"

"Not sure. She loves the arts and knows a lot about it. I've considered asking her to become part of my staff, however, I'm not sure I'm going to be the owner much longer."

"What do you mean?"

"Jax has been inquiring and I'm about set to move on to another project. Of course he'll need me to stay on until he can find a permanent replacement as director of the gallery."

Freda smiled just as Tess approached.

"Yes, Roldolpho, you needed me?" Tess asked.

"Come sit a moment. I have some questions for you," Roldolpho said, and Freda listened in as Tess explained all that she knew about Sparks. Freda looked down below again as Tess prepared to head back to work. She caught sight of Sparks as three men engaged in conversation with her.

"Sounds like she's hard up for money. All those college loans, that rent, and finding a full-time job. I feel terrible," Roldolpho stated.

Freda touched his arm and squeezed it. "I told you that she was interesting. Let me handle this."

Roldolpho stared at her with eyes squinted.

"What are you up to, Freda?"

Freda smiled. "Just giving a little push where a push might be needed."

"Hmmm…sounds delicious. Can't I join in the fun?"

"I promise to let you in on it and call you if I need backup."

"Oh backup! Sounds sexy and makes me think of muscular, naked men wearing firearms and ready to play rough."

Freda laughed then shook her head.

"If all goes well, there will be some serious action and perhaps fireworks, too," Freda said, and Roldolpho clapped his hands and laughed with excitement.

* * * *

Jax knew that he was probably scaring her, the brunette who snagged his attention entirely. He was watching her and she noticed. The moment those hazel eyes locked onto his, his cock hardened and his need to have her exploded. It was fucked up. He never got like this, or at least not instantaneously. *Who the hell is she?*

"Sparks, can you grab another platter in the kitchen for the second floor? Roldolpho needs you?" another young woman said, and it hit him. *Sparks? Is this the same Sparks in the sweatshirt on the skateboard?*

His mouth dropped as he looked her over and she practically bolted for the kitchen. She bumped right into Clover Masters. Clover held her arms and stared right down into Sparks's cleavage.

"Hey, beautiful, where's the fire?" he asked and pressed her against the wall. She looked toward Jameson and then up at Clover.

"I need to get to the kitchen."

"I was looking for you. I wanted to tip you personally," he said then pulled some rolled bill from his pocket as he leaned against her. She looked freaked out as Clover pressed the money down her blouse.

Jax was fuming, and something came over him as he crossed the room in three strides and pulled Clover away from her.

"Give her space," he practically growled at the man.

"What the hell, Spaulding? Find your own piece of ass," he said, and before Jax could react as a small crowd of people looked on, Jameson was there as he grabbed Masters by his shirt collar and placed his arm behind his back in an aggressive manner.

"Apologize to the nice young woman," Jameson demanded.

"Sorry, sorry!" he yelled, and then Jameson released him. Masters gave them a nasty look then walked away.

"Are you okay?" Jameson asked Sparks as Jax joined them. She pulled her shirt tighter.

Jax felt angry, and one look at Jameson and he could see how close his brother came to slugging Masters.

"I didn't need your help. Either of you," she said, but looked upset. Jax was pissed off and wanted to grab her and demand to know her real name and everything about her. He ran his hand through his hair and tried to fight such possessive feelings for this stranger. Jameson touched her hand. She looked down at where he held her wrist and then back up at him.

"Are you sure that you're okay? I saw him press something to your chest," he said, sounding hesitant.

"I'm fine. I appreciate your help. Sorry if your evening was ruined," she said in a somber tone then walked away.

Jameson and Jax watched her enter the kitchen.

"What the hell?"

Jameson looked at Jax. "I don't know how you didn't knock his lights out. Fucking Clover Masters is such a dick," Jax stated.

"He had no right to touch her. She'd be defenseless against a guy like him."

Jax saw the anger in his brother's eyes, and his own emotions mirrored them.

"I think we need to find out who she is," Jax stated very seriously and hoped that his brother was on board.

"Definitely," Jameson said as they turned to look for Roldolpho.

* * * *

It was the end of the evening, and Mariana was exhausted and feeling like an emotional mess. Those two hot guys totally threw her for a loop when they came to her aid with that snobby dick Clover Masters. He was such an asshole and everyone knew it. He also couldn't hold his liquor. She saw him bombed at numerous parties, and he always hooked up with some dumb-ass chick screwing him for his money or to say that they spent the night at his huge penthouse. *Who cares?* So why was she still thinking about those two men, Jameson, and Tess said the brother's name was Jax? Brothers.

How the hell can I be attracted to two brothers? Not that it's uncommon for a relationship like that, but me? I don't even trust men, why would I double my bad odds? They are really good looking. The one appeared rugged and untamed despite his dress shirt and designer pants. The other one, Jax, was a total dominant boss. Not that Jameson seemed wimpy at all, he just seemed more reserved about his masculinity. Jax appeared instantly superior. Definitely out of my league. Men like them don't date. So why am I so aroused and interested sexually?

"Excuse me, Sparks, is it?"

Mariana nearly jumped, slightly off guard at the voice coming from behind her. She turned around to see Freda Mulsberry, a quadzillionaire or something like that, standing behind her. She was dressed so beautifully, a woman in her sixties, adorned in fine jewels and with her own bodyguard who escorted her everywhere. Mariana never met the woman but had served at enough parties to hear about the woman's money and achievements.

"Yes, how may I help you?" Mariana asked, and the woman smiled.

"The name is Freda Mulsberry. It's nice to meet you, Sparks?"

"That's what everyone calls me. It's nice to meet you, too, Ms. Mulsberry."

The woman smiled.

"Please call me Freda."

Yeah right. How's it going, Freda? Want to hang out sometime and you can show me your collection of people you own? Mariana chuckled to herself. She shouldn't just assume the woman was a stuck-up rich snob just because the majority Mariana had met were.

"Won't you join myself and Roldolpho for a bit? I have something to discuss with you," she said as she looked her over. Mariana got a funny feeling in her belly. She hoped that the lady wasn't into some kinky shit and wanted her to participate. It wasn't like she hadn't been asked to do some crazy shit at some of these big-shot parties. She lost a few future jobs because of her declining.

"Don't worry, honey, it's nothing bad. No indecent proposals or anything like that."

Can she read minds?

Mariana chuckled then glanced at Tess who shrugged her shoulders, and Mariana walked away with Freda.

They walked into the private office, and Roldolpho was there and he was pouring some cognac.

"Such a good job as always, Sparks. I hope Clover didn't hurt you," Roldolpho said, and she felt her stomach drop. He was going to fire her. Oh shit, she lost her job because she wouldn't let some dick wad feel her up, and those two other men had their time ruined because of her.

"I'm so sorry, Roldolpho. Please don't fire me. I'll make it up to you."

"Whoa, darling, what are you talking about? I'm not going to fire you. None of that situation was your fault. Clover Masters is a dick with legs and even I, who personally like dick, hate him," Roldolpho stated very femininely with his hand on his hip and the other one snapping his finger in a zigzag motion. Freda covered her mouth and laughed loudly. Mariana stood there in shock.

"Come sit down, Sparks. Is that really your name?" Freda asked.

"It's Mariana actually."

Freda smiled.

"Mariana. Such a beautiful name."

"Very beautiful just like her," Roldolpho said, and she felt her cheeks warm.

"So, I have a bit of a proposition for you?" Freda began to say and then proceeded to tell her about her escort service. By the time Freda was done talking, Mariana was feeling overwhelmed but interested.

"I explained to Freda about your immense knowledge of the arts. I was considering discussing with you the possibility of employment here, but seeing as I may not own the place for much longer…"

"What? Is someone trying to buy you out?" she asked.

"In a way. That's not your concern. I think you should consider Freda's offer. She is completely legit and has emergency assistance in place if needed."

"Does this mean you're taking me off the list as a server for the parties here and elsewhere? You were my connection to other events?" Mariana asked as feelings of dread filled her body. How was she supposed to pay her rent and her college loans? She needed her courier job and this one. "I don't think that now is the time to take this risk. I already work two jobs. I barely make ends meet for food and stuff."

Both appeared shocked, and she was embarrassed for admitting that.

"I'm fine really. I'm not desperate or anything. God, I'm sorry, I don't know if this is right."

She felt Freda's hand cover hers, and when she looked up, Freda was smiling.

"Not to worry. I haven't discussed payment. You see, my girls, the ones who work for me as escorts, get paid very well for what they do. There are contracts the men have to sign beforehand and I know most of them very well or they have been recommended by other clients. Considering your expertise in the arts, I am certain that your services will be needed for very elite art events at both private and elaborate establishments."

"Like at the Rothesburgh gallery?" Mariana couldn't help but ask.

"Yes, or even at private estates," Freda said with a smile.

"Depending on the event, you can get paid by the hour or by the evening. Three hundred dollars or three thousand dollars or more for the entire evening."

Mariana gasped. She was utterly shocked, and then it hit her. This was a trap, a scam, and she would have to put out, she just knew it.

She crossed her arms in front of her chest and squinted at Freda.

"I have to have sex with these men if they want it, don't I?"

Freda raised her eyebrows at Mariana.

"No. You do not have to have sex with them. It is not that type of escort."

"What if they want to or they try to make me? "

"You have a panic button per se. If you're feeling threatened or concerned for your safety, just hit this button and someone will be there to assist you immediately."

"How can that be? I mean, is someone escorting me secretly?"

Freda smiled.

"Yes. You are never truly alone. It's part of the fee these men have to pay and it ensures me that my girls are safe. There are others just like you who are trying to pay for school or even help their families out. So what do you say?" Freda asked.

"I guess I'm in. I need the money and you mentioned that if I don't like it, then I don't have to do it again."

"Yes, exactly."

"Okay, deal," Mariana said then thrust out her hand for Freda to shake. Freda smiled and shook her hand.

"Wonderful. Let's celebrate. To finding love and happiness despite the storms a-brewing." Roldolpho toasted.

"What?" Mariana asked.

He shook his head. "Forget it and let's drink."

She had a funny feeling in her belly. Something told her that this decision might just change her life.

Chapter 3

Jax and Jameson were standing in the main office at X-Caliber. They had their small staff, and everything ran so smoothly that neither man really spent much time there. They were usually in the field, confirming that proper procedures were being followed or personally running surveillance. Jameson spent a few days working in the lab at home with new ideas to help protect fellow soldiers with updated technology that cost very little to make. "So why are we here today? What is this all about?" Jameson asked as he leaned back onto the front of Jax's desk.

Jax smiled then looked at his watch.

"Just two more minutes," he said as the buzzer on the desk went off. Jax smiled as he pressed the button.

"Let 'em in," he said in response to his secretary stating that a package arrived.

The door opened and Jameson locked onto the kid in the skateboarding outfit. He wore sunglasses, a knit hat, and tight jeans with elbow pads and kneepads.

But then the kid gasped and he realized that it wasn't a boy, it was a girl, and then it hit him.

"Sparks?" Jameson said as Jax walked behind her and closed the door. She stood there with a package in her hands and nibbled her bottom lip.

Jameson looked at Jax then back at Sparks.

Jax crossed his arms in front of his chest and stared down at her.

"Take off the glasses," Jax stated very firmly, and Jameson knew that tone. Jax was in commanding mode and he wanted this woman.

Hell, Jameson wanted her, too. She was all he could think about the last few days since the party.

"No," she whispered.

"Do as he says, please," Jameson added, and she released an annoyed sigh. She stepped forward and placed the box on Jax's desk. Slowly she pulled off her sunglasses. Her cheeks were flushed, but her face was gorgeous, just like he remembered from the other night.

She pulled out a slip of paper and pointed it toward Jax. "Can you sign this please, Mr. Spaulding?" she asked with a bit of attitude, and Jameson wondered why she was annoyed with them. They had come to her rescue the other night when that asshole tried to touch her.

"Call me Jax, Mariana," he whispered, and Jameson felt his chest tighten and Sparks looked shocked. Was that her real name? Mariana?

She took an unsteady breath as Jax moved closer. He reached for her knit hat as he held her gaze.

When he pulled the hat off her head an abundance of gorgeous brown curls cascaded over her shoulders. Jameson's eyes widened.

"You're stunning, Mariana," Jax said then held her hat as he reached toward her face and twirled a curl around his finger. Her lips parted, as she stood there appearing so innocent and delicate as an angel.

"What do you want?" she asked softly.

"You," both Jameson and Jax responded together. Jameson looked at Jax, and they stared at one another a moment. It hit Jameson hard but in a totally good way. His brother wanted to share Mariana. Holy shit, their discussion years ago in the desert was going to become a reality.

Mariana stepped back, grabbing her hat from Jax in the process.

"I'm sorry, but I'm not interested."

Jameson instantly felt fear and an almost panicked feeling consume him.

"We want to get to know you," Jameson said as Jax encroached on her space again.

"No. I need to go. I need this job," she said as she reached for the doorknob.

"When can we see you again?" Jax asked as he pressed the palm of his hand against the door so she couldn't open it. She stared up at him. Jameson could tell that she was fighting an attraction as she stared up into his brother's eyes. She was just scared. Of course she was. She looked so young.

"I'm not that kind of woman and I'm not interested," she said then stuffed her thick locks of brown hair under the tight knit cap.

"Please, just leave me alone." She pulled the door open and started to head out. Jameson felt his gut clench. He had an overwhelming urge to stop her, but he didn't want to scare her. If she wasn't interested, then that was that. The thoughts made him feel defiant, as something inside him roared "no."

"I'll just ask for you to deliver something else again tomorrow," Jax pushed. He was always so persistent. He stood tall, looking down at sweet, petite, Mariana. Jax found out her real name. What else did his brother find out?

"I'm not interested," she stated again and walked out. They both watched her as she picked up her skateboard with a stomp of her foot. It flipped up, and she caught it and headed toward the elevator.

Look back, Mariana. Look back and let me know that you're even the least bit curious.

A slow turn of her head as she glanced over her shoulder made Jameson feel triumphant. *This isn't over. In fact, Sparks, it's only just begun.*

They walked back into Jax's office and he closed the door.

"Damn, Jameson, even in fucking skating pants and looking like a boy, she's hot," Jax said as he ran a hand through his hair. Mariana got to him. Jameson never saw his brother like this.

"What's next?

"Whatever the cards throw our way. If I'm right, then she'll be back here sooner than later. Or, we see her at the Rothesburgh on Saturday night. She'll probably be serving food."

"I hope so. She felt the connection or at minimum an attraction to both of us. Does this mean what I think it does, Jax?" Jameson asked with his arms crossed in front of his chest and a dead stare into his brother's eyes.

"We're going to find out. All indications point to a shared relationship with her. I don't know about you, but my dick is fucking hard. Never, and I honestly mean never, has just meeting a woman made my dick this fucking hard. I want her. I want to touch her, explore that sweet little body of hers, too. You know I always get what I want, Jameson. And if you want her, too, and feel what I'm feeling, I'll get her for both of us."

"Jesus, Jax, she's not some toy. She's a person, she's sweet and seems so innocent and shy."

"I've seen her toss the bird to a guy behind his back. The woman has a temper on her if pushed too far. I didn't mean to come across like some pompous rich asshole. All I'm saying is that, she's going to take some convincing. Maybe's she's been hurt before."

"Hurt?" Jameson felt his temper rise and defenses instantly go up.

"I don't know, but I'm going to find out. Shit, Jameson. This is what we do for a living. We identify the mark, initiate a plan, organize an assault team, and we go in and get that mark. We need to be patient."

"You're telling me to be patient? You're the 'I want it in an instant' guy. I'm the patient one."

"Yeah right. I saw you. You wanted to reach for Sparks, pull her into your arms, and kiss her until she complied with our demands."

Jameson raised his eyebrows at him then shrugged his shoulders.

"Her name is Mariana. How'd you find that out?" Jameson asked.

"It wasn't difficult. I also found out what company she works as a courier for, obviously. I asked for her to deliver any packages from now on."

"We don't get much from couriers."

"We will now. Anything that can ship through that company and that is small enough for Sparks to carry will be delivered by her to us," Jax said with a very serious expression on his face. Jameson knew his brother well. He was a boss, a leader, and commander even out of the Marines.

"Okay, so I guess this means I'm forced to go to another one of Darian Rothesburgh's parties at his gallery. Do you think that obnoxious cousin of his will be there? She can't take no for an answer."

Jax chuckled. "She did take no for an answer the last time."

"Her hand was down my pants. There was no warning. She jumped on my lap and shoved her hand right in there. In front of a crowd of people."

"It was a sight. But you handled it well?"

Jameson raised his eyes at his brother as if questioning his recollection of the events.

"Hey, you didn't toss her over the couch or onto the floor."

"I almost did. Instead I eased her grip off my dick then grabbed her by her wrists and placed her on the side of the couch beside me."

"She wasn't wearing any panties, you know?" Jameson teased.

"Yeah, not my kind of woman."

"Nor mine, but it did make for a nice chuckle later on."

"I think I swore I wouldn't attend that gallery again, come to think of it."

"You're going, Jameson. Keep your eye on the target. We need to figure out if she's the one."

Jameson thought about that a moment as Mariana entered his mind. He needed to know more about her. He thought about how she brought over those appetizers he had asked about. She didn't have to do that. Besides, she actually didn't even flirt with him. It was like she did it just to make him happy. How come there wasn't a catch? Maybe they were both wrong and maybe Jax and Jameson were the targets. Trust didn't come easy for Jameson, and now this whole situation just a got a bit more crazy.

Chapter 4

Mariana unlocked the door to her apartment. The moment she did, she knew that there still wasn't any heat working in the crappy apartment. She closed the old door that always had a draft and locked both locks, including the one she installed herself after the multiple muggings and assaults in front of the apartment building.

She shivered. She was tired, hungry and—*damn, I forgot to hit the store.*

She threw her bag and pack onto the small beat-up sofa that came with the apartment. Turning on a light, she looked at the thermostat and shivered some more. *Forty-seven degrees? Shit, this is going to be a cold night again.*

The thought of taking a hot shower and washing her hair was all she imagined on the bus ride home. Now, she would be shivering when she got out. Plus she had a test to study for.

Mariana was feeling the stresses of her daily routine. She looked into the refrigerator. *Yogurt or yogurt?* There were only two left and both were the same flavor, strawberry.

She shivered again, grabbed the yogurt, and closed the refrigerator as the cold air made her feel worse.

She washed her hands with warm water, letting the hot liquid ease the ache from her frozen fingers. She would need gloves to sleep in tonight. Layer upon layer, she wasn't going to get a good night's rest.

She grabbed a spoon then headed toward the couch. She wrapped a throw blanket over her shoulders then sat cross-legged on the couch. She didn't dare remove her sneakers yet. Her feet would freeze.

Opening the yogurt, she sat back and tried to relax her aching muscles. She had had a lot of deliveries today after school this morning. But one delivery stood out from the others. The one to X-Caliber Enterprises. She gulped down the spoonful of yogurt, instantly feeling her belly tighten. This was not a good dinner by far. She finished it off in no time at all then sat back and thought about how hungry she still was. The cold air penetrated through the thin blanket and she leaned back, closing her eyes wishing she were someplace different.

Instantly she saw herself between two men. Jax and Jameson. She knew it was them as she tried her hardest to make the images stop. This was happening to her all day today. Every time she had a moment to think or to close her eyes to rest, she saw them. One was kissing her shoulder and the other cupped her face between his hands. She could practically feel the warm breath against her lips. She could tell even with eyes closed that both men were big, much bigger than her, and strong, too.

The images in her mind would switch. One moment it would be Jax, and his dominant stare held her in place. He was a man of power and control. His clothing, his clean-cut face, and firm mouth and jaw spoke volumes. He was a man not to reckon with and a man who got what he wanted. So why was she so turned on by that? Men with money and power were evil and manipulative. They would never take a woman like her in her current position seriously. Then she thought about Jameson. Oh God, was he so damn sexy, too. Either man could stop traffic. She was on the receiving end of some vicious eye daggers when she left their office. Every woman in the place stared at her with hatred. She swallowed hard. Jameson seemed so sad the other night. Yet today, he looked different. He seemed determined or something. She was attracted to him, too. That was what made her panic. They of course came right out and said they were interested in her. Yeah, great, just what she needed, two wealthy men who liked to play games and who wanted to play with her at the same time.

She gasped as a small bit of cream dripped from her pussy. She placed her hand over her belly as her mouth gaped open. Did she just react like that? She slowly pressed her fingers past the waist of her pants to her panties. As she felt the dampness, her breasts perked up and her nipples hardened. She closed her eyes, and Jax and Jameson filled her thoughts. She felt her swollen clit. It felt hot and sticky. She was shocked and then came the annoyance. She pulled her hand from her pants and stood up abruptly tossing the blanket onto the couch.

She wasn't going to jerk off just because two hot sexy men wanted to have sex with her together. She wasn't interested in that or in them. Men were pigs. She learned that. She wouldn't play their games no matter how good their lines were or how hot and excited they made her feel.

She pulled clean clothes from the one small dresser in her tiny bedroom. Tossing the stuff onto the bed as she looked for her extra-heavy hoodie sweatshirt, she couldn't stop the sensations running through her body or mind.

She felt needy. She was lonely and annoyed with her life. Mariana knew that she was attracted to the two brothers. Today in their office she practically moaned at the way Jax stared down into her eyes. She shivered at the darkness of his blue eyes. Jameson's matched his, but Jameson looked ready to cause anarchy or be wild. That thrilled her inside.

"Stop it. Stop thinking about them and making them into something you can't have," she stated aloud as she held her head and tried desperately to stop their images from appearing.

She grabbed her clothes and headed to the shower realizing that she no longer felt cold but entirely too hot for a woman standing in a fifty-degree apartment all alone.

Stay away from the Spaulding brothers. They'll hurt you worse than Gavan did.

* * * *

The rest of the week seemed to have flown by. She was pleasantly surprised to receive a package at work when she signed out for the night.

"Who is it from?" she asked Al, her boss. He wasn't exactly a friendly guy, but he paid on time.

"Some guy dropped it off. That's all I know."

She waved good night then headed out of the office. She was curious as to what it would be. She never received any packages, or mail, at her apartment. It wouldn't be there when she arrived anyway. People stole constantly. She didn't even use the mailbox at the apartment complex for that reason. Instead she kept a box at the courier's office and only because Al let her have it for five dollars a month. But she usually only got bills. She felt anxious about the box. Maybe it was a mistake? Who would send her something? She couldn't wait to see as her curiosity had the best of her. She had never meant anything to anyone before. At least not enough to send her a special box at work. She released an annoyed sigh. *Why am I getting teary-eyed? It's just a damn box and probably a mistake.*

Sitting down on the bench outside the office, she began to open the box. Inside was a note then something covered in purple paper.

She opened the note and was pleasantly surprised to see that it was from Freda Mulsberry. She welcomed her to the business and told her she may have an assignment. She followed with instructions including meeting her tonight at Sassy's. That was a top-of-the-line dress store uptown. The sound of a cell phone ringing made her jump. She realized instantly that it was coming from under the purple paper. She undid the paper and saw a very high-tech cell phone. That was a luxury she could never afford. She assumed she was to answer it and immediately took the call.

"Hello?" she asked hesitantly.

"Hello, Mariana. So wonderful to hear your voice. So I see you got off at the time Al said you would and that you received my package. Very good. Now I need you to walk outside. My driver, Benny, will take you to meet me at Sassy's. Time is of the essence," she said.

"Okay," Mariana hesitantly replied then heard the phone click.

Her driver, Benny, is here for me? Excitement, reservations, and other motions filled her.

She gathered the box and paper, tossing it into the garbage nearby. She took the phone, wanting to be sure to give it to Benny or to Freda when she saw them. She thought about tossing out the note from Freda, but something made her hold on to it. For some strange reason she felt like her life was about to seriously change.

She walked out of the building with butterflies in her belly and her backpack slung over her shoulder. Sure enough, there was a black stretch limo. Before she even made it out of the building and to the sidewalk, an older gentleman got out from the driver's side and immediately welcomed her.

"Miss Sparketta, I'm Benny, your driver."

"Hi, Benny," she replied, feeling completely awkward. Especially since some workers began to exit the building and saw her now.

"Shall we?" Benny said then opened the back door to the limo. She stepped inside and her mouth gaped open.

The car was huge and luxurious. There were fancy crystal bottles of liquor, an ice bucket, and multiple types of crystal glasses.

Benny got into the driver's seat and spoke to her from the rearview mirror.

"If you're hungry, Miss, there are some small sandwiches in the refrigerator and some bottles of water or soda."

"Oh, thank you," she replied, and he began to pull away from the curb and head into traffic. Her belly was in knots. She was nervous, excited, but also starving, and once again, she hadn't had time to stop at the grocery store. She located the small refrigerator that was hidden behind the matching black trim she thought was part of the fancy cabinetry.

The assortment of sandwiches was amazing. She chose one along with a bottle of water and chowed it down quickly, knowing that Sassy's was only a few blocks away. Just as she finished up, easing the ache in her belly somewhat, they arrived. The limo pulled into an underground parking garage she didn't know existed. When they parked, Benny got out and led her through the garage to an elevator.

"Just take the second door on the right. Mrs. Mulsberry is waiting."

"Thank you for the ride," she said, and Benny smiled then tipped his hat at her before heading back to the limo.

As she made her way to the door, she had some reservations. She was taking a chance here. She didn't know any of these people. Was she becoming so desperate for a better life that she was taking such a risk like this? What if Freda wasn't legit? What if she operated a prostitution business or something? As the panic set in, the door opened and she immediately recognized the man.

"Good evening, Mariana. Mrs. Mulsberry is waiting."

Her bodyguard escorted Mariana into another room and then the back room to Sassy's. There stood Freda, wearing a velvet jumpsuit in black and sipping champagne with a very beautiful woman in a red dress.

"There she is," Freda said, and she walked over, grabbed Mariana's hand, and hugged her.

"Isn't she beautiful, Margarete?"

"My God, she's stunning," the woman said as she looked Mariana over.

"I'm wearing skinny jeans and a sweatshirt," Mariana replied to their comments, as she felt really awkward.

"Nonsense. I've seen you dressed up before. You're gorgeous and it's natural beauty. Now, meet Margarete. She is the owner of Sassy's."

Mariana was in shock. Freda must be loaded.

"So Mariana, you've attended some of these art events before. You know how the attendees dress and conduct themselves. I don't believe you will have a problem with that at all," Freda said then smiled.

"No, ma'am. In fact, I've often dreamed of attending the events as a guest and having ample time to view the art and really see some famous originals close up."

"Well, you are going to get your chance. I know you're going to do fabulous and Margarete is going to help you look the part," Freda stated and Margarete smiled. Mariana clasped her hands and took a deep breath as she anticipated what would happen next. Margarete and Freda went back and forth about colors that would suit Mariana and certain styles. They weren't quite arguing but it did seem as though the women knew one another well.

But as the evening went on, she came to realize that Margarete and Freda were actually friends and she designed many of Freda's gowns she wore to fancy events. They went through the clothing, everything from undergarments to hair accessories and products.

She felt incredibly spoiled and completely uncomfortable. Especially as Freda told her she was taking this home. Her apartment was bad, and if anyone saw her bringing anything inside, their curiosity would bring trouble her way. But how could she explain this to Freda?

* * * *

Freda was enjoying this time with Mariana. She was such a sweet and quiet young woman, and she adored her immediately. But something seemed to be bothering the woman. She became awfully quiet.

"Margarete, could you give Mariana and I a few moments alone please?"

Margarete smiled as she touched Mariana's shoulder before leaving the room.

"Sweetheart, is something wrong?"

The poor woman looked ready to cry.

"I can't accept these things from you, Freda. I can't pay you back and I don't have a place to keep them."

"Nonsense. You don't have to pay me back. It's all part of working for me. I enjoy this and especially when I know how much it is appreciated. You can't go out and start buying the wrong outfits. I have a reputation to keep and an image to stand by."

"You don't understand. I do appreciate all of this. I can't even begin to imagine how this is going to work."

"But?"

"But, my apartment..." Mariana lowered her eyes to her hands. She was shaking, the poor girl.

"What is it? What's wrong?"

"I live in a really shitty neighborhood. If I walk in with anything I'll be targeted. It's bad there, Freda, but it's all I can afford."

Freda was immediately concerned and upset. How could this beautiful young woman live in such a dangerous place? She couldn't tell her to move in with her. Mariana was different. She was a fighter. She did things on her own. She needed to tread carefully here.

"Listen, I'll hold these items at my place. On Saturday, you have your first assignment."

"What?"

"Yes, you're going to need one of these dresses Margarete picked out for you and, well, since I am actually attending the same event, I need my beautician there and assistant. So, I will have Benny pick you up at your apartment at three tomorrow. You'll get ready at my place and I will have everything there for you."

"You really don't have to do that."

Freda covered Mariana's hand with her own.

"I want to. You'll learn quickly that I only do what I want to, not what others want me to do. Now, give Benny your address and he will pick you up."

Marianna shook her head.

"I can meet you at your place tomorrow. There's something I need to do first."

Freda wasn't sure if Mariana was lying or not. She would have Alvin follow her to ensure her safety.

"Okay, dear. Benny will give you my home address."

Mariana said "thank you" as Margarete reentered the room holding a gorgeous black cocktail dress with sequin overlay. It was stunning, and Marianna would look incredible.

"Oh God, that is amazing," Mariana said, and Margarete smiled. "This dress, you will wear to Rothesburgh Gallery tomorrow night."

"Rothesburgh Gallery?" Mariana gasped as she stood up, took the gown from Margarete, and placed it against her. Freda could hear the excitement in her voice. Mariana loved the arts and she would be the perfect escort for Liam Michaels III.

"You will look amazing in that, Mariana. So meet me by three o'clock tomorrow and we will go over all the details of your assignment and what will be needed of you."

"It sounds so mysterious. I can't believe that I'm going to the Rothesburgh," Mariana said as she turned to look at Freda. Freda smiled.

"It will be a great evening and your date for the night is practically royalty."

Mariana's eyes widened as Freda grabbed her purse and asked Margarete to have everything delivered tomorrow morning by noontime.

"Wait, you can't tell me something like that and then not say a name," Mariana said as she gently handed the dress over to Margarete. Margarete laughed.

"She shouldn't even have said so much already. I think Freda is as excited as you seem, Mariana."

Mariana blushed and Freda put on her coat.

"Margarete is correct. Escorts shouldn't know whom they are escorting until the night of. However, in this case, you may need to brush up on your knowledge of Scottish artists."

Mariana smiled. "A Scot, huh? Very interesting."

"You'll see. We'll go over everything tomorrow."

"Thank you, Freda. I'm nervous and excited."

"You'll be perfect, and after tomorrow night, I'm certain you will be giving up that courier job and serving at parties. You're going to be quite busy."

Freda waved good-bye as Alvin opened the door for her.

"Oh, Alvin, will you give Mariana a ride home?" Freda asked then left before Mariana could reject the offer. She was worried about her and where she resided. How could the poor young woman live in a place where people stole so blatantly? She sighed in annoyance.

"Are you okay, Freda?" Alvin asked as he opened the door to the limo with Benny standing there.

"Just worried about Mariana. I want you to give me an update on her living arrangements tomorrow, okay?"

"Yes, of course."

Freda stepped into the backseat as Alvin leaned down to speak with her. They locked gazes and she knew he had something on his mind. He was a great man and he always kept her safe.

"She is quite lovely. Not just a project, I hope."

She smiled.

"Not a project. She's special and I have two specific men in mind that need a woman like her in their lives."

Alvin shook his head and chuckled.

"Since when did you become a matchmaker?"

She folded her hands on her lap and stared up into Alvin's big blue eyes.

"Since I witnessed their first meeting and saw the immediate attraction between her and these two men."

"And how do the two men feel about this?"

"They haven't a clue nor does Mariana. You'll see, Alvin. These three are meant to be together. They just need to get through some of the walls they've built up over the years. I love a challenge," she said, and he smiled.

"Yes you do, Freda. Good night."

He closed the door, and Freda left for home with Benny driving. She thought about Mariana and how lovely of a woman she truly was. Now, she needed to find out about Mariana and what type of past she was hiding.

Chapter 5

Jax was on the phone with Spider. He was a fellow Marine and now worked for their company as a main investigator whenever Jax or Jameson needed him. Aside from that he was the director of operations for their security firm, X-Caliber.

He was trying to process all the information as he spoke with Spider and looked over the e-mail and documents he forwarded to Jax.

"Son of a bitch. This is a lot to digest," Jax stated.

"It's a lot to have found out about in a matter of days. But it's important to see the signs that this asshole wants to fuck with you."

"Spider, I'm not too worried about Clover Masters. He may have some political contacts but that doesn't mean shit to us commandoes. He wants to try stealing from my brother and I, then we'll take care of it."

"He's got these people in place. The word is someone is working on the inside to duplicate Jameson's new ideas. Which is telling me that this snitch is close to both of you."

"I don't know who it could be. Jameson rarely works with staff at headquarters."

"It could be someone who has access to your computer correspondence. That would be the simplest way to steal the graphics on the new products. Perhaps it's time to do some computer overhauling and place some tracking devices in position."

"Do it. I don't want this to blow up in our faces. These are my brother's ideas. How about you? Any inkling as to whom the rat might be?"

Spider was silent a moment which made Jax feel like his good friend was on to someone.

"I have my suspicions. I'll work my magic, Jax. I'll nip this in the bud before it blows way out of control."

"Good. So, what else do you have for me? I see three more attachments on the second e-mail?"

Jax opened up the files.

"That's your woman."

Jax clicked on the first file. He wasn't surprised that it contained an entire background check on Mariana. Twenty-four years old. *God, she's young and gorgeous.*

"She's a beauty, Jax. I feel bad for her actually."

"Why is that?"

"You two are quite the handful and that young woman has led a pretty tough life. It's impressive actually that she doesn't have a rap sheet."

"What do you mean?"

"Her mom, Adele Sparketta, was arrested numerous times for prescription drug possession and buying. On the records from the police department and on file, I found out that Mariana bailed her out each time. You'll see all the documents. I got everything I could get, as you asked."

Jax sighed as he opened up the attachments and looked them over. Spider wasn't kidding when he said he got all the information he could on Mariana. He had her previous home addresses, her grades, her college application, and student loans.

"Holy shit, she owes a lot of money."

"Her mother took a loan out on the house they lived in to support her habit. Mariana is still paying that off, too. It's sad when you think about it. That woman is trying to get her college education and she has all those bills, including her mother's, breathing down her neck."

"This is unbelievable. Wait, this can't be right. This is her current address? She lives in that crappy neighborhood?"

"Yeah, unfortunately that is accurate. I watched her come in last night late. She looked exhausted."

"Did you see her place?"

Spider was silent a moment.

"Spider, I asked you if you saw her apartment?"

"It's a fucking icebox. Literally. I got in no problem. The locks are shit, although she did have an added bolt lock on there. Self-installed, I think. It's really small. One bedroom if you want to call it that. There's only enough space for a couch and tiny kitchen. There wasn't any heat in the place when I was there. It was fucking cold. But she's neat. Nothing was lying around."

Jax felt his gut clench. She was living in a shit hole apartment with no heat and there was a damn cold front in Houston right now. He wanted to get to her, and make her come home with him and Jameson. Fuck! Jameson was going to freak out.

"So she seems organized."

"I don't think she has much, Jax. The bare necessities from what I could see. I didn't want to overstep my bounds, but there was only one dresser in the place that had undergarments and clothes. The closet was basically empty. If she owns a dozen outfits for all four seasons, that would be a lot."

"Fuck! Son of a bitch, I don't like this."

"Hey, she's tough, that's for sure, and seems determined to have a better life."

"I appreciate all the info. I'll be in touch if I need anything more in regards to this. Keep me updated on the other issue."

"Will do, Jax."

Jax hung up the phone and thought about Mariana as he looked at the computer.

* * * *

"You look upset. What's the problem?" Jameson asked his brother as he entered the office. Jameson was fixing his bow tie. He hated formal events like this. It made him feel fake.

Jax looked at the computer screen and explained that Spider had called about Clover Masters's plot.

"That piece of shit. I'll fucking rip his throat out."

"Calm down, Jameson."

Jameson felt his blood pressure rising. Clover touched Mariana the other night at the party. That scumbag was a wannabe.

"Who does Spider think the rat is?"

"He thinks it may be anyone close to us or who has access to our computer system. You know e-mails and correspondence between you and I and the staff."

"I'd hate to think that there's someone stealing from us. We treat our employees so well. This is the shit I'm talking about, Jax. I'm not a patient or forgiving man. If there's a rat, I want him or her exterminated."

"I feel the same way. I trust Spider to handle it though. He and his brothers have a way about them."

Jameson nodded his head even though he wasn't feeling so confident right now. He was a man of action. If someone messed with him, then he would mess them up. It was that simple.

Jameson looked at his brother, who was already dressed in an almost identical tuxedo. They both wore custom-made black-on-black tuxes. The cuffs to the black designer shirt under the jacket were white. Jameson closed them with diamond cuff links that his brother had insisted looked amazing and was the proper way to wear a custom tux. Jameson could give a shit.

He stepped to the side and immediately saw Mariana's picture. It looked like a crappy ID picture and was slightly blurry.

"Is that Mariana?" he asked.

Jax looked at him, and the moment Jameson locked gazes with his brother he could see he was thinking of what to say.

Jameson moved around the desk, and Jax began to explain. Jameson could feel his concern for her grow stronger. It was amazing, but Mariana had remained on his mind since meeting her. He wasn't sure how he felt about the fact that Jax had Spider investigate Mariana, but at least now he had a better understanding of her reservations.

"No wonder she seemed to shy away from us. She probably thinks we'd use her. God knows how many men have come onto her at those parties she serves at. How do we get her to see we're different?"

"I thought about that."

Jameson nodded toward the screen.

"Scroll the mouse down. What does it say about her family?"

Jax explained about her mother. Jameson took a deep breath and slowly released it. How could a mother, responsible for a child, act in such a way?

"Where does she live?"

"You don't want to know."

"Yes, I do."

Jax released a sigh.

He brought up the address and some pictures Spider sent along with the info. Spider was thorough.

"That neighborhood is bad." Jameson stood straighter and began to pace the room.

"What did he say about it? Did he check out her apartment?" Jameson asked as he placed his one hand on his hip and stared at Jax.

"Bad."

"Fuck!"

"Tell me about it. I'm freaking out right now, Jameson. I'm trying my hardest to not act like a psycho stalker and follow her myself to ensure her safety. I can't do that. We can't do that."

Jameson ran his hand through his hair. "No fucking heat? That shit is against the law."

"I know it is."

Jax remained staring at Jameson. It was as if they were both communicating without speaking. Jameson nodded his head.

"It can't hurt if she doesn't know it's us."

Jax smiled.

"I think Rudy Jones works with the housing committee and development. He would know how to get to the landlord and how to get that damn heat turned on."

"Make the call, Jax."

Jameson walked out of the room.

It was too much to take in. His mind was going off in crazy thought patterns. He closed his eyes as he thought about how sweet and pretty she looked that night at Roldolpho's. He thought about the way she got him those appetizers he asked about and it wasn't because she expected something in return. She did it to please him. Instinctually that fed his male ego. Knowing a bit about her past and her struggles, it made him want to do something for her, too. God knows he'd seen enough violence and death in the Marine Corps to know how lonely a person could feel. He hadn't been quite the same since he got out of the Corps and after the death of so many friends.

Then he thought about Clover Masters and how he stuck his slimy fingers next to Mariana's breast to tip her. That fucking pig. If he ever came near Mariana again, he'd be in huge trouble.

Jameson felt his blood boiling as he made fists by his side then tried to calm himself down.

"We need to get going. We're already late as is."

"Tomorrow, we get another package delivered."

"Tomorrow's Sunday," Jax replied as he fixed his bow tie and grabbed the keys to the Lexus.

"A visit to her neck of the neighborhood may be in order, don't you think?"

"That sounds like something I would do."

"We're both men who get what we want when we want it. You, however, sometimes choose things that aren't needed. I'm simple," Jameson teased.

"Yeah right, you're simple. You've got a short fuse and you're very protective of what you believe to be yours."

"So do you, Jax. That's why this idea about a ménage relationship came to mind. We know how a relationship like this works. We've witnessed the energy between multiple partners. The question is, whether our independently strong personalities can survive sharing the same woman or if it will place a wedge between us. That's my concern," Jameson admitted as they entered the elevator to head downstairs to the car.

"The only way to know is to try it."

"At risk of hurting Mariana? I'm not sure I can be so cruel."

"Cruel? What are you talking about? You're attracted to her just as I am. There's something more there. Call it instinctive, but it's there. My heart is racing. I'm worried about her safety now, her well-being, her future, and it's making me antsy to see her."

"I'm feeling the exact same way. I'm feeling possessive and she isn't even mine or ours," Jameson added.

"I have a plan," Jax said as the elevator door opened and they walked out and then down a corridor to the parking lot. As they exited, the Lexus was parked close by. He unlocked the car and Jameson got in on the passenger side. Jax started the engine.

"What's you're plan?"

"Shock and awe her. I want her very badly. In fact, I'm glad I won't see her tonight. If I did, I might have done something crazy," Jax admitted, and Jameson was feeling the same way.

"Crazy like what? Because I'm thinking I would lose it as well and this taking it slow and easing our way into her life would be useless."

"We're not going to see her there. She's probably working at another event."

"Or she's working at Rothesburgh. No other gallery would dare have an event when the Rothesburgh estate was hosting the Scottish art exhibit."

Jameson clenched his teeth and imagined seeing Mariana there serving.

"This evening might not be as boring as I anticipated."

Jax held a wicked smile as he headed out of the building and onto the highway.

* * * *

Mariana drank down the glass of champagne quickly. She needed it for her nerves. Here she was at the Rothesburgh estate. The mansion that was worth well over fifteen million dollars was outrageous. She tried to remember every detail she could upon arriving with a hunk of a date, Liam Michaels III, who just happened to be Scottish and wearing a kilt. Bless her pounding heart, the man was fine, but also in his forties. He was built magnificently and she memorized everything about him. From his sexy accent to his deep-green eyes and very defined cleft in his chin. He was tall, sexy, and a total gentleman. On the way over to the estate from Freda's mansion, which was incredible, Liam explained about his business dealings and his love of Scottish art. He was somehow related to a person connected to the Royal Scottish Academy. Therefore, he had access to new and seasoned artists of his native country.

"Are ya ready ta browse now, Mariana?" he asked in that sexy Scottish accent that did wonders to her belly.

She smiled and nodded her head. He escorted her around the exhibits until they paused in front of a series of paintings from new artists she wasn't aware of.

"Ahh, it's always nice ta see some new blood coming into their own. What do ya say 'bout this one, Mariana?" he asked, and she felt his arm around her waist and his large hand on her hip. He was acting awfully strange. She knew she had a bit of a role to play, but he was acting like she was more than a date. He whispered into her ear. He ran a finger along her collarbone.

"These are nice, however, I can see the way the strokes of the brushes are harder, almost forced. Can't you, Liam?" she asked, turning up toward him as she moved slightly to place some space between them.

He was staring down into her eyes.

He placed his fingers under her chin and tilted it up toward him.

"I am in awe of your beauty, Mariana. You are a pleasant surprise," he whispered then began to lower his mouth toward hers. She quickly turned away and stared at the picture. He gave her a bit of space.

"I'm sorry. I was out of line. I know that this is not in the contract. I've never hired a date before, but I do have people I am trying to impress with business. As you know. Please forgive me." He was stumbling with his words, and she felt terrible. It seemed he was not used to doing this kind of thing either.

She looked up at him and smiled.

"There is nothing to forgive. We seem to both be caught in the ambiance of this estate. The beauty of all this spectacular art is like—"

"An aphrodisiac?" he teased, and she felt her cheeks blush.

"Are we back to that, Liam?" she retorted. Then he chuckled as he took her arm and continued to walk with her through the gallery.

* * * *

"And whom did you say that is with her?" Jax asked Roldolpho, who had joined him and Jameson by the exhibit. Jameson noticed Mariana immediately, and they thought their prayers were answered.

Watching her walk along dressed like a fucking model and holding hands with that Scottish man had him filled with jealousy. She looked gorgeous, and they weren't the only men to take notice of her. Who was that man she was with? Never mind whom he was, he wasn't going to be leaving with Mariana tonight.

Jax looked at his brother who was in a dead stare at Mariana and the Scot.

"I'm going to go find out who that is," Jax stated.

"No need to. That's Liam Michaels III. He's visiting from Scotland."

"Why is he with Mariana then?"

Jax felt the hand touch his arm and then Freda's soft voice.

"Because she's working for me now, Jax. She's quite stunning, isn't she? I can just imagine all the requests I will get for her."

"What? When the hell did this happen?" Jax asked, raising his voice and nearly causing a scene, but he didn't care. Mariana was not going to be an escort. That would mean men touching her, holding her hand, escorting like a piece of jewelry all around Houston. No, not happening.

"I spoke with her that night I saw her at Roldolpho's. She is so sweet and very knowledgeable on the arts. She has natural beauty, don't you think?" Freda asked with a smile, and then Darian Rothesburgh approached to greet them.

As Darian exchanged pleasantries, Jameson locked gazes with his brother. Jax could see his brother losing his cool. Hell, he was losing it, too.

"Need another drink? Or perhaps we should browse the artwork since that is why we are here," Jameson stated to Jax. They excused themselves from the conversation and walked toward the direction they last saw Mariana headed.

* * * *

"This place is huge. How many people live here?" she asked Liam.

"I'm not sure. I don't believe more than three," Liam replied as they stared at a daguerreotype of John Wilson Ewbank.

"Liam, so nice to see you here. The board is happy that you were able to attend."

Mariana turned as she saw four men join the conversation. These had to be the business people Liam wanted to impress.

"Thank you, Marcus. This is quite the display of Scottish art. I feel right at home," Liam said as he shook the men's hands. His Scottish accent was so cool.

"Wonderful. And who is this lovely young woman you've brought along with you?" Marcus asked as he reached for her hand and Liam made the introductions.

The four men stared at her body and she felt embarrassed. She was never one to flaunt her assets, but after receiving the royal treatment at Freda's, she looked completely different. Her hair was styled in a fancy updo and the dress was slim fitting and accentuated her hips, her ass, and of course her breasts. Not that there was a low dip to the front, but the cut of the dress accentuated her breasts in such a way that it was very sexy, yet not too revealing. Margarete knew how to pick out the right dress for the right woman. Mariana was even getting used to the high heels, too. Freda had made her feel like a princess, and she was hoping this night didn't fly by so quickly.

"So this right here is a nice photograph taken by a well-known Scottish photographer, I believe," Liam said, and the men turned to look at another picture with a famous person they surely would recognize.

Liam gave Mariana a squeeze and she took her cue as the other men, two with Scottish accents, made comments about the photo taken by a famous photographer, Albert Watson. They walked closer.

"It is quite impressive for such a simple pose. But I bet you didn't know that Albert Watson thinks of this as one of his favorites," Mariana began to say.

"Do tell, my dear. It sounds intriguing," Marcus said and took position beside her. She was surrounded by the four men as she told a bit of the tale around the photograph, which here, was blown up into poster size.

"Well Mr. Watson was extremely excited to photograph Alfred Hitchcock. It was his first celebrity photograph," Marian said.

"Why the goose?" one of the others asked.

"Well, from the story Watson tells, he finds out in casual conversation that Hitchcock hunts goose and is quite a good shot. You see here how he chose to take the photograph with Hitchcock holding a plucked goose?"

"That's risky," Marcus said.

"Not really. Watson believed it to be more natural because of Hitchcock's hunting experience. That was a twenty-five-pound plucked goose that he's holding like that. Watson tells a story about how Hitchcock gave his Christmas goose recipe to all the people working on the photography site. They enjoyed the shooting immensely."

"Intriguing," Marcus said, and then the other gentleman pointed to a series of other pictures. They walked along, and she hadn't even noticed the small crowd that seemed to gather around them as Mariana explained about each photograph she knew of and the artist's behind-the-scenes stories. She loved doing this. She enjoyed bringing people into the minds of the artists from the artist's point of view.

"This has been the best event I've attended, Mariana. It was such a pleasure meeting you," Marcus said as he took her hand then brought it to his lips and kissed it. She glanced at Liam, who looked very pleased, and she felt relieved. Perhaps her first job would be a successful one.

"Can we take Liam for a few moments, Mariana? We have some business to discuss."

"Of course. Please take your time," she replied, and Liam took her hand and gave it a squeeze. He leaned down and whispered into her ear, tickling her skin.

"You are a gem. I will see you in a little bit."

She smiled as he walked away. She felt her body warm and then a tingling feeling moved over her skin. She looked toward the right where she knew a series of John Wilson Ewbank paintings were on display and locked gazes with Jax.

Oh my God, he looks so sexy in that tux. He's all in black and appears mysterious and intimidating. I'm in trouble.

It was strange how her body just knew that he was nearby. The tingling sensation, that warm heat that skimmed across her skin. It was him. He caused that.

She debated about turning around and heading the other way, but she didn't. He was too good looking to ignore and in all honesty, dressing like this and playing this role gave her confidence she normally wouldn't have.

When he smiled slightly at her, she felt it to her gut. She also felt a tiny spasm in her pussy. How the hell did he do that?

"Mariana, you are in a lot of trouble, young lady," he said as he reached for her hand. She hesitated, and he took control immediately, pulling her alongside him. He was pressed close to her. He towered over her as he inhaled against her hair.

"I've been waiting patiently to speak with you. It seems you've snagged the attention of every man in this place tonight."

Why did he sound so angry and bossy? What was his problem? Hadn't she been clear the other day at his office?

"You seem upset."

"Who is he?" he asked abruptly.

She felt her body tighten and nearly shake with a combination of excitement from his demanding tone and fear that she was completely out of her comfort zone with Jax. If Jameson showed up, she was toast.

She stepped back and began to walk toward the enclave of displays, set back in a more private and secluded location. She could handle this. She handled bill collectors hounding her all the time and uptight college professors who thought she was ignorant and too young to understand the arts, so she could handle one such business man who reeked of wealth and commanded compliance.

She swallowed hard.

"Liam is from Scotland," she said as she tried to focus on the coastal scene in front of her. Of course it had to be one of Ewbank's more tragic depictions, but she forced her heart to stop racing and straightened her spine. But then she felt the hand on her waist. Large, hard, yet gently en route around her waist, he wrapped her firmly.

She gasped as she felt his solid chest against her spine, his cock, hard against her ass despite the barrier of clothing, and then the warm breath of his whisper.

"I don't give a fuck where he's from, he wants to take you home and that's not happening."

His words were so firm and so damn macho she hadn't expected her body's reaction. She should be angry, turned off, or at minimum shocked by his possessive words. What gave him the right to say such a thing to her?

She swallowed hard again, and this time her saliva nearly got caught in her throat.

"I'm a big girl, Jax. I can take care of myself." She hated that her voice cracked, because as she said those words, he used his free hand trail a finger along her neck then pressed his warm, solid lips against her skin.

Holy fuck, this man is amazing. Fight it. Don't be so easy. He's a professional, he has to be, wearing a tux like this and cuff links made of what is certain to be real diamonds bigger than I have ever seen before. Things like this do not happen to regular nobodies, like me.

She tried to step away, and he released her. She was both disappointed and relieved. She needed to gain control of the situation.

He took her hand. His thumb caressed along the top of her skin, causing goose bumps to explode across her flesh.

"This is quite the painting. The roaring sea swallowing up the helpless, foolish swimmers."

She felt his breath collide against her shoulder and neck where the skin was exposed.

"Why do you think they're foolish?" she asked and shocked herself for coming up with the coherent words at all.

"For challenging the sea."

She absorbed the sight of the painting of the seascape from the east coast of Scotland. Large, wild waves smashed against the rocks. Ewbank made the people so small that they appeared quite miniature in comparison as they struggled to grab any bits of items left over from the boat wreck.

"I suppose it does show how powerless man is against forces of nature," she whispered.

"It's interesting, because this painting sort of reflects the way you make me feel."

What in God's name did he just say?

His hands moved up and down her arms, caressing her skin.

"Mariana, I know we don't know one another well yet, but I want to change that. Please say you'll have dinner with Jameson and I tomorrow night."

In her mind she wanted to accept. Her body never felt strung so tight and so interested in such a fantasy, but she wasn't as naïve as he might believe.

She stepped to the side and turned toward him. Jax stared down into her eyes, and she fought against the superior aura of his presence and stature.

"I'm not naïve like the people in that painting. I would never venture into the unknown as you are asking me to. I couldn't even if I wanted to. Not when there's so much to lose and I'm not one to take risks with what little I have."

She was about to walk away when Jameson appeared. His arms were by his sides. He seemed angry and stiff. Was he jealous because she was talking to Jax and alone with him? She couldn't help the thought. These men weren't really interested in a ménage or what it was meant to offer. They were in it for sex.

"Where'd the Scot go?" he asked so forcefully she found herself stepping backward, and Jax pulled her back against his chest.

"Oh," she gasped, and Jameson's eyes seemed to darken with excitement. Perhaps she was wrong. Perhaps these men really did get turned on by sharing a woman. Could she be that woman? *Are you fucking crazy? Snap out of it, Mariana. They will eat you up and spit you out. They're rich.*

"He's going to be back any moment. You two should go," she said and tried to act tough as she pulled from Jax's hold. Well, tried to pull away. Her body apparently liked the sensation of being practically encased in such arms that she stumbled. Jax squeezed her to him and Jameson closed the space between them. He looked her over. His body was inches from her own, and damn it, she could feel the massive heat and attraction. She wouldn't need heat in her apartment if she had Jax and Jameson.

She shook the idiotic thought from her mind.

Yeah, sure. Bring the two rich hunks who probably live in a mansion to my dinky shit hole apartment. They're treating me like a whore. As quickly as she had the thought, she denied that Jax or Jameson were like that. But it still didn't mean she was taking them home or that she would go with them.

Jameson touched a finger to her chin, tilting it up toward him. She felt Jax's cheek move against her cheek and his thick, solid arm of steel hold her around her waist.

"Get rid of the Scot, and come with us."

She shook her head.

Jameson gave her a look that told her that he wasn't used to being told no. Jax's grip loosened as he moved in front of her. Now both gods stood in perfect position where she could truly absorb their fine features and muscular builds. They were a woman's fantasy. She knew they were, because right now, even looking them over fully clothed, her panties were wet and her nipples hard.

Men like this should be illegal.

"Mariana?" Jameson said her name. She looked away.

"Please don't do this to me. I'm not like that. I won't sleep with you because you demand it or want it."

"It's not like that. I said that I wanted to get to know you. So does my brother," Jax stated as he held her hand and gave it a gentle squeeze.

"Mariana! There ya are. I thought I lost ya for good." Liam appeared, and when he saw Jax and Jameson so close to her, she could tell he was upset.

"Liam, did everything go well?" she asked, stepping away from Jax, who hesitated to release her hand. Liam looked down at it and then into Jax's eyes.

"Is there a problem here, Mariana?" Liam asked as he took her hand and pulled her to him. Thank goodness Jax released his hold.

"No problem. These are friends of Freda's. Meet Jax and Jameson Spaulding."

"Jax and Jameson, meet Liam Michaels III, my date this evening," she added then smiled and looked up at Liam. He gave her a wink and then squeezed her against him.

"It's a pleasure, gentlemen. Thank you for watching over my woman in my absence. I've heard about ya security firm. My new partners speak very highly of ya abilities."

"Thank you," Jameson squeezed out through clenched teeth, and Jax looked none the better.

"Well, Liam promised me a tour of the estate after we grab a bite to eat. Enjoy the evening," Mariana said, and Liam escorted her away from Jax and Jameson.

* * * *

Clover Masters was standing by the bar sipping a cognac along with his partner Buster McShay.

"I think we should pull back. There have been some glitches in the computer communications. She can't seem to bypass the new passwords," Buster said to Clover, and he seemed awfully nervous and unsure.

"That was when mistakes happened. She was in a rush and now I think they may be on to the breach in security."

"I really don't care. It's not even like I need the money or the details to Jameson Spaulding's new ideas. I'm loaded," Clover said in a very snobby manner. He was in his early fifties, in great physical condition, which helped him to land the younger ladies, and he hated Jameson and Jax Spaulding. With a passion.

Ever since Rothensburgh's cousin Tara took a liking to Jameson he hated the man. So what that he and his brother were ex-military. Didn't bother him any. He owned a few senators.

"So why are you risking so much? Revenge for something?" Buster asked then took a sip of his cognac as they watched two very attractive women walk by. Clover didn't respond to Buster as his eyes locked on the beauty in front of him.

He spotted her immediately. That woman was stunning and she had been serving hors d'oeuvres at Roldolpho's last week, and now here she was attending as a guest? He followed her with his eyes as the large Scotsman linked his arm through hers and led her to the dining area. A quick glance toward the staircase they descended and he was surprised to see Jameson and Jax Spaulding. They looked very angry and their eyes were locked on the brunette.

"Find out whom that woman is with the Scotsman. They seem jealous don't you think, Buster?" Clover asked as he downed the remainder of cognac and fixed his tux.

"I'm on it."

Jameson and Jax followed the brunette and her date. Something was up, and if both men were this agitated over a woman, then that woman would be of great interest to find out about.

Clover suddenly felt like his revenge could be successful after all.

* * * *

Mariana and Liam got something to eat then took their glasses of champagne with them as they toured the home. It wasn't much of a home in regards to warmth or coziness. Instead every room, every hallway that led to another room or area, was wide and rather cold. It made her feel like she was in a museum. But then they headed toward the left wing of the house, and that was when she met Darian Rothesburgh himself.

"Darian, this is a wonderful gathering. I've enjoyed all the artwork from my native country. Ya sure know how ta make a Scot feel at home"

"That is wonderful to hear, Liam. And Miss Sparketta, such a pleasure having you in my home. I've heard such wonderful things about you."

"Me, sir? It's an honor to meet you."

He took her hand and brought it to his lips as he held her gaze. "Simply stunning. Hold on to her, Liam, she has caught the attention of many bachelors." He released her hand then excused himself as he headed out of the room.

Mariana blushed. She was so embarrassed.

"He may have a point and I might have to keep you for myself," Liam said as he squeezed her to him. They heard someone squeal, and immediately Mariana and Liam turned toward the entry way a distance from where they stood and saw Jameson and Jax as some woman in a tight blue dress threw herself at Jameson. Mariana watched as the woman wrapped one leg around Jameson's thigh and he held her around her tiny waist as she hugged him hard around the neck. Mariana was surprised at the surge of jealousy that exploded through her system. She hadn't even realized that she clutched Liam's arm tighter or that she was staring daggers in Jameson and Jax's direction until Liam cleared his throat.

She locked gazes with Jax, who appeared annoyed, and Jameson? Well, Jameson she couldn't see, under the flowing blonde locks of hair, as the bimbo kissed him deeply. *Why does she remind me of Bambi, who took Gavan from me?*

"Unbelievable," she stated aloud as she turned and Liam led her out of the room.

She didn't dare look behind her. Mariana couldn't take the scene. She was right. They were both players and she was supposed to be on their menu tonight. *Jerks.*

So why was she feeling so disappointed the further Liam and her walked through the estate? Why was she upset, hurt by that scene?

Suddenly Liam stopped her from walking and pulled her into a small hidden space next to a set of large windows that looked over the gardens.

"You're upset."

She needed to snap out of this. She was working, not socializing. This was a job and this wasn't her lifestyle. She wasn't cut out for all the backstabbing and two-faced nonsense.

"I'm okay. I'm sorry if I was so quiet. Would you like to see some more artwork? I understand that they have some paintings from Vettriano and Kingsley."

He shook his head as he leaned back against the wall and stared at her.

"What is it, Liam?" she asked, feeling a bit unsure of herself. He sure did get quiet, and now they were completely alone.

"I wish, that I would find a woman who looked at me the way those two men looked at you. And I wish that you would look at me the way you looked at them."

She swallowed hard and tried to deny what he was implying.

"I don't—"

He placed his finger gently over her lips and then patted her hand.

"My darling woman, they adore you and you adore them. So why are you running from them?"

"Liam, I don't know what you mean. I don't know Jameson or Jax at all. I know nothing about them."

"But they make your eyes sparkle and fill you with energy and excitement. It's plain as day to see."

"No, no way. I don't know them. Besides, you saw that scene back there. That was what I was afraid of. This is not me, Liam," she said as she pointed to her outfit and then wrapped her arms around herself. "I don't belong here as anything more than your date for the evening."

He raised his eyebrows at her, and she raised hers at him. He chuckled.

"Come on, let's go see that artwork." She accepted his hand as he led her out of the hallway and back toward the gathering. But he whispered to her as they walked and she imagined for a moment, if things were different, if she weren't such a nobody, would Jax and Jameson pursue her at all?

"You know, things aren't always as they seem, Mariana. Sometimes risks are worth taking, even if only for a moment of pure bliss." Liam squeezed her hand, and she wondered, *Why can't I be attracted to Liam, instead of two very dark, mysterious, and dominant men who seem to make me want things I've never even dreamed of trying?*

She would dream of their touch, the intensity of their eyes, and taking a chance that could kill her inside and ruin her life entirely. She couldn't allow those dreams, those fantasies to make a decision for her. Life was not a movie, a scene in a painting, a magical experience. The realities of life sucked. Bills, death, loneliness, and battle after battle were all part of her life. Once she got through all of that, perhaps she could focus on happiness after survival.

Chapter 6

Mariana dressed in her plain old clothes. A pair of old blue jeans, a hoodie, and her sneakers. She looked at the gorgeous dress one last time before zipping up the garment bag. A glance around the elaborate bedroom in Freda's home and she was in awe once again of the lifestyle some people got to live. She looked into the mirror, the amazing sophisticated-woman act she pulled off tonight now disappeared back into the pumpkin. No more makeup, fancy hairstyle, or expensive jewelry. Everything was placed back where it belonged, and last would be her.

She needed to head home. It was nearly two in the morning, and she had a test to study for. The reality of life, her life, was breathing down her neck and crashing against her chest. She felt the tears emerge. She wanted more, she was fighting for more, but she had to stop thinking that she would ever fit into a world like this one.

Mariana grabbed her backpack and dinky jacket. It was cold outside but still colder in her apartment. The warmth of this room, the large king-size bed, and all the lovely accent pillows looked so appealing. She wished she could lie down and rest here and not venture out into the cold and to her small cave of reality.

She swallowed hard then opened the door and began her departure down the long hallway. There were gorgeous pictures both from artists and from photographers.

She reached the winding staircase, a picture perfect home out of a magazine of mansions. Freda was a lucky woman.

"There you are. Are you certain you don't want to spend the night? It's no trouble at all," Freda said as she stood at the bottom of the stairs.

"Oh, I couldn't do that. I'm fine, really."

"It's no trouble at all, Mariana, really," Freda said. Her blue eyes sparkled, and she looked so nice and motherly. *She's not your mother, idiot. Your mother was a drug addict and a loser. This is not your world.*

* * * *

Freda could see the emotional struggle Mariana was going through. A quick talk with Liam, who was very impressed and taken by Mariana, uncovered some interesting information. Mariana was young, she was quite resourceful, and definitely was interested in Jameson and Jax. Any fool could see the attraction between the three of them. But this woman had fears, uncertainties, and Freda was learning what those were.

"Perhaps another time then, you could plan on staying. We could have breakfast together. I'm forced to eat alone so often with Derrick, my husband, gone."

Mariana looked up at her, and she suddenly looked sad. That wasn't Freda's intention at all. Especially after Alvin told her where Mariana had gone before she arrived here this evening for her first date. The poor girl visited the grave of her deceased mother. Yes, things were beginning to become quite clear to Freda.

"I'm sorry, perhaps another time, Freda. I don't want to impose or be a bother. What you've done for me is quite beyond the norm of what a boss does for their employee."

Freda smiled.

"You are special, Mariana. Even Liam noticed that about you."

Mariana smiled.

"He was a very nice man and handsome, too. I enjoyed his company. So, I should get going. It's late and I don't want to miss the bus and wait another hour in the cold."

"Oh, Benny is going to drive you home, dear."

"No, that's okay. You've done so much." Mariana began to head for the door.

"Mariana, honey, I know where you live. It's nothing to be ashamed about. You're trying to pay for college."

The poor woman looked so sad and about to cry, Freda felt terrible.

"You know, how? Why?"

"I have to investigate all my employees. Alvin knows where you live and he reported back to me."

"I'm some sad charity case for you? Is that why you offered me the job and why you brought me to Sassy's and brought me those things?" she asked, and Freda could tell she was insulted and hurt.

"That wasn't my intention at all. You need to look and dress the part. Not you, nor any of the women I hire, have the funds to do so without my assistance. It's something I need to do but also enjoy doing. Don't for one moment think of yourself as a charity case. Now, it's late, you live in a crime-infested neighborhood, and Benny is going to drop you off and walk you up to your apartment."

"Not in a limo I hope. We'll never make it to the front door," Mariana said as she nibbled her bottom lip. Freda smiled then took her hand.

"Not to worry, dear. Oh, and here is your pay for the evening. I more than likely will have another job for you by Saturday. A small event at a private home outside of the city. I will let you know."

She handed over the envelope, and Mariana blushed. She was so gracious and sweet. For a moment she feared that Jax and Jameson might eat her up alive. They were dominant and masterful. Any woman Jax had ever been with was submissive and he could be rough. She heard different stories, but who knew what was true? Their sex lives didn't matter to her as much as their hearts. They were good men. Men who made it through battle then struggled to achieve respect and greatness in their professional field. They had come so far and proved that hard work and commitment won out in the end. Mariana was so much like them, but she was doing it alone as opposed to having a brother to lean on for support.

"Thank you, Freda. I have the cell phone, so call me when you know. Thank you again," Mariana said, and then she leaned down and hugged Freda, shocking her.

Freda watched her go, and for a moment she wondered what it would be like to have a daughter. Derrick was sterile and they couldn't conceive their own child. They made the decision to be alone, but now in her sixties and with Derrick gone so suddenly, she wished she had a child to spend time with. The tears filled her eyes.

"Freda, are you okay?" Alvin asked as she stood in the doorway to the sitting room. He had been there the entire time without anyone knowing. He was her bodyguard and her friend.

"Just thinking about life, Alvin, and how things turn out differently than planned. You know, seeing Mariana, it makes me wish Derrick and I had adopted children."

She walked toward the stairs and held the railing.

"Mariana is quite the young woman, Freda. You've done so much for her. I've never seen you like this before."

She turned to look at Alvin. "I'm just being silly, Alvin. I know I'm destined to die alone. It's the way it must be because of those choices Derrick and I made so long ago." She started to head up the stairs when she felt Alvin take her hand to stop her. She looked at him with tears in her eyes.

"You're not alone, Freda. I'm not planning on going anywhere."

She smiled, touched by his commitment and loyalty to her.

"Thank you."

"If I might be so bold to point out, Freda, perhaps Mariana is in need of fulfilling a similar void in her life and maybe the two of you could lean on one another. After all, we know where she went before she arrived here today in preparation of her first job."

Freda understood completely and nodded her head, feeling a spark of hope fill her heart. She was a patient woman, and she knew firsthand that sometimes things happen for a reason.

* * * *

Mariana was completely surprised to have Benny pull up in front of her apartment complex in a Range Rover and see all the utility vans. They were working on something.

"Oh God, maybe there'll be heat tonight," she said aloud as Benny parked the car behind one of the vans.

She opened the door before he could and he locked it then escorted her inside.

"Are you having problems with the heat or electricity, Mariana?" Benny asked as they entered the building and saw men working.

"I haven't had heat all week," she said, and now Benny looked upset. But as they climbed the stairs, she could feel the warmth like never before in the building.

"Oh God, I think the heat is on. It's never been this warm in here," she admitted then took out her key to unlock her door.

"Thank you for the ride, Benny. It sure did beat the bus and walking in the cold." He looked a bit angry, and then his expression quickly changed and he smiled.

"My pleasure, Mariana. Call me if you need a ride anywhere. I'm on automatic dial in your cell phone on number three." He winked then began to head back downstairs. She was still embarrassed as she unlocked the door and the heat hit her instead of the pinch of icicles.

She locked her door and smiled as she closed her eyes and tightened up her body. She had to remember this moment, this evening, this experience forever. It was the first bit of happiness she felt in such a long time. As she opened her eyes, she threw her backpack onto the floor near the couch and began to pull off her jacket, as she remembered the envelope of money. She opened it, and her mouth dropped as she fell to the couch.

"Oh my God, two thousand dollars?"

Her mind raced as she thought about this type of work. She could do this. She could make this kind of money doing something she enjoyed, and she didn't even have to have sex. *Holy shit!*

She jumped up and twirled around her small apartment thinking that if she could do this, she could put a dent in those college loans and that damn bank bill that came every month. She was so excited and felt a bit of relief and hope that she could slowly begin to dig herself out from under the weight of debt, and she thought of Freda. She owed her so much. The woman truly was an angel, and perhaps one day she could repay her in some way that would truly let her know how much Freda meant to her.

She smiled knowing that tonight she would go to bed warm and happy for the first time in ages.

* * * *

"We need to do something, Jax. I'm not going to stand by and let other men touch her, escort her around galleries and parties as if she belongs to them. We have to make her see that we mean business," Jameson said as he ran his fingers through his hair.

Jax wasn't surprised by his brother's words. He felt the exact same way. They hadn't slept well at all Saturday night or Sunday night. It was Monday, they were in the office for a few hours now, and all both of them kept thinking about was Mariana. At least they knew she hadn't left the party with Liam to go to his hotel. Not that Mariana was like that, but they didn't trust Liam or any other man with their woman. God, those words stung so hard. She wasn't theirs yet, but she would be.

"I'm thinking, Jameson. I agree with you, we discussed this for hours, remember."

"This is insane. You're the one who always takes what you want. I've seen you with women, Jax. You dominate, you control and demand, and they comply. This situation is going too far."

"She's not like those other women, Jameson. She made that clear Saturday evening. I thought we were making progress until Tara showed up."

"God, that woman is an animal. She had no boundaries whatsoever. She attacked me. You saw her. I couldn't stop her fast enough. I kind of felt badly for telling her that I would never be interested in a woman like Tara but it had to be said. She recovered quickly though. Did you see her with that guy in the hallway?"

"I was there Jameson and I saw how Tara attacked you, but so did Mariana and, man, did she send daggers our way. But that's a good thing."

"A good thing. How could you say that, Jax?"

"Because, she looked pissed off and jealous. From there on out, the rest of the evening she really played up being with Liam. We know that she's an escort and that was a business job. There was nothing to worry about."

"I'm not too sure. Liam looked very interested, especially as he kissed her good night."

"It was on the cheek, Jameson."

"He touched her, he hugged her, he pressed his lips against her skin. Fuck!"

Jax pulled out his cell phone. "You're right. We need to take action."

Jameson watched as Jax began to talk with Freda.

"So you want to book up all her Saturdays for the next three months?" Freda asked, and he could hear her shock.

"Yes. Jameson and I would like to lock in on her available dates of service. We have a busy schedule ahead of us."

"I can arrange this if you are certain, Jax. I'll need deposits on these. I was actually going to call you to see if Jameson or yourself were available as guards. I have three men scheduled for dates with her and they aren't regulars. If you can't handle this—

"Not a problem. We can handle security for her. Just name the nights. But also send us a contract for her available dates and we'll send the deposit. We need her this Friday and Saturday."

"Oh, I'm sorry, Jax, her first availability isn't until next month."

"Next month? What? How? She just got started," Jax asked in shock, and he looked at his brother who had his fists by his sides.

"She made quite a wonderful impression Saturday night. I have some heavies calling to book her. You're actually the tenth person who called this morning. The phone started ringing on Sunday. She's going to be busy. As a matter of fact, I need to call her and see how her schedule with work and school is for this week. There's a special event on Thursday night. Oh, I'll have to call you back, Jax. I'll pencil you in for Saturdays starting next month and I'll have Alvin call you to talk about what dates she needs security for."

"Wait, Fridays, too, remember?"

"Not certain I can do that. I need to go, Jax. I'll let you know. Bye." Freda hung up, and Jax stared at his phone in shock.

He slammed the cell down on his desk and they both heard the crunch of plastic.

"What? What does she mean a month?" Jameson asked, and Jax explained. Now he was angry.

"That's over ten dates, ten men that will hold her, hit on her and try to—"

"I know," Jax interrupted through clenched teeth.

Chapter 7

Theo Centurion from Centurion Estates, an elite art gallery in Houston, was standing alongside Mariana at the premiere event. This wasn't a bad job at all. She immediately noticed some familiar faces, and Theo was very busy speaking with so many people. She was more on display as his date than anything. Here and there he called her over to explain more about certain pieces to those people pretending to be interested in buying. She was shocked, though, mid evening as one man purchased an original Jack Vettriano painting for eight hundred thousand dollars. He wrote the check on the spot, and no one even questioned his ability to pay. She couldn't imagine having so much money and being able to purchase fine paintings as a collector. Mariana hoped to one day run or even own a gallery. In some aspects, running a gallery and choosing what art to display for a time being would be like having the ability and means to purchase. Even if it were for a short time.

Mariana was walking through the study, where some more paintings by Vettriano were displayed. The guests were eating dinner and Theo was entertaining the buyers, so she had some free time to herself.

As she made her way into the quiet room, she had the opportunity to look at some of the well-known paintings by Vettriano. There was *The Singing Butler, Dancer in Emerald, For The Dead Admiral*, and then the more provocative of paintings that immediately drew her in.

She stared at the painting called *Lovers and Other Strangers*. Immediately her mouth went dry and a feeling of awareness or maybe even arousal perked her body's attention. Especially her nipples as she absorbed the figures on the painting and the way the sexy, masculine man held the woman with such control.

Deep down, Mariana knew she was submissive in nature. In public she could be assertive to an extent and in class when she raised her hand to give the answer or had to make a public presentation. But looking at this painting that she always found to be so sexy made her think of things she really shouldn't entertain. There was an almost invisible pull as she stared in awe. It told a story, as far as she believed, and involved the sexual attraction between two men and one woman. Not so far fetched and more prominently written about, besides being a subject of many artists.

In this particular painting, Vettriano painted the picture of one man holding a woman firmly around the waist. The palm of his hand pressed snuggly against her flat belly as his other hand began to unzip her dress. The most erotic part was the image of a man sitting in a large cushioned chair, watching. He was wearing a tux and holding a cigar whose smoke silhouetted upward toward the couple as he watched.

In her mind she imagined Jameson and Jax. Shocked at how easily she saw herself as the blonde in the picture, head down, accepting to the one man's touch as the other looked on. She wasn't an exhibitionist. She liked her privacy and held in a lot of information about herself. She preferred it that way. But oh, how nice it would be to be able to let go completely, and know that she was safe.

The moment the arm came around her waist, for real, she gasped and turned to see Jax standing there.

"One of my favorites, too," he whispered, and her heart began to race. He mimicked the position like the man in the painting. His arm was snugly wrapped around her center. Jax's other hand lay flat against her side, his fingers inches from the swell of her breast.

She tried to speak, but a squeak came out so she cleared her throat. This man made her so damn nervous.

"You look stunning this evening, Mariana," he whispered then kissed her shoulder and trailed more tiny kisses along her neck. She was lost in the sensations of his touch and the feel of being this close to him. Her mind yelled for her to place some distance between them, but it was too late. The painting, the memory of last week of how fine both Jax and Jameson looked in their tuxedoes, ruled her mind all week.

"Jax, please, I'm here with someone."

His hold grew tighter a moment, and then he eased up. It was as if he was angered by her statement.

"I know, that's why Jameson and I are here. We're keeping an eye on you," he said then kissed along her neck some more. When she felt his fingers tangle in her hair and hold firm, she found her body reacting in an unexpected way. Her lips parted, her eyes closed, and his hand smoothed across her belly. She was utterly turned on.

The realization of his statement hit her. He was running security? He was the guard she needed for the date tonight because Theo Centurion was very wealthy and had enemies.

"Please, Jax, I need to go."

"Not yet. I'm mad at you."

She opened her eyes as he eased his hold on her hair and wrapped both arms around her, pulling her against him.

"Mad at me why? What have I done?"

"Appeared in a setting around people who want you, but can't have you because you're ours, Mariana. When will you realize this?"

His words sounded so final and hard. She didn't know if she should feel frightened or flattered. This was not normal behavior. She needed to think about this. She needed to understand what it was that she wanted. Jameson and Jax both confused her.

"I need to go."

She turned from his embrace only for him to pull her against his chest. He ran his hand along her waist and her rear. Placing his palm against her ass, he squeezed.

"This is not over between us. Jameson and I want time alone with you. To talk, to discuss these feelings."

She gripped his forearms, immediately feeling the stone and muscle beneath her palms and fingertips. He was a fit man and resourceful. He was her security, and for some reason it turned her on, just like everything else had in the last ten minutes. She nervously licked her lips, and a moment later Jax was kissing her. She tried so hard to resist the urge to kiss him back and take advantage of this wild moment. But it was no use, he tasted so good, and it felt amazing to be held in his arms. He explored her mouth in smooth, gentle strokes until she began to pull back. It was too much, too wild. She didn't know him.

Then the kiss grew deeper, wilder, and she felt her body react on instinct. Her nipples pebbled, her belly tightened, and her legs began to shake. Then she thought she heard a bird whistle or something. Jax eased up then gently rubbed along her bottom lip as if fixing her makeup. He glanced over his shoulder, and she followed his movement and locked gazes with Jameson. He looked fierce, dressed in black and in a dead stare at her.

"Theo is coming here looking for you. Jameson and I will be in touch. Be good, Mariana," he whispered then tapped the tip of her nose gently with his finger as he smiled.

She watched him walk away as Jameson looked at her with an expression as hard and fierce as stone.

A few seconds later, as she tried to calm her racing heart, Theo arrived.

"There you are. I need you to come with me. I have some business associates I'd like you to meet and also explain a bit about some paintings."

She smiled as she took his hand and he led her out of the room and back into the reality of her life.

* * * *

Mariana had just walked out of the ladies' room when she heard the voice behind her.

"I've been waiting for you. Theo asked me to accompany you to the study. He has some clients who are interested in a painting and they would like your input."

Mariana hesitated a moment. She didn't recognize the man at all. He was stocky, had dark hair, and was a few inches taller than her. He appeared angry, but she wasn't certain if that had anything to do with his bushy eyebrows. If Theo sent him, who was she to question it? Mariana followed him down the long hallway. She glanced over her shoulder, noticing that no one was in sight, not even Jameson or Jax. God, why was she even thinking about them? She couldn't. They were a weakness she wasn't ready to face.

The man glanced back at her, and she got a funny sensation in her belly. It just didn't seem right at all.

The moment they entered the study, she was on guard. The man waiting there she recognized as a buyer of fine art. His last name was Ellington. No, his first name was Ellington and last name James. It was like his name was backward. That was how she remembered him.

Her hand instinctively went to the small broach by her waist. It appeared as accent jewelry, but it contained a tiny button that would alert her security person that she was in trouble. She cringed just thinking that it could be Jameson or Jax. Here she was trying to act so independent and confident. She didn't want Jax or Jameson to think she needed them or would call them unnecessarily just to see them again. She couldn't press that button unless she was in trouble. Big trouble.

She cleared her mind and focused on the situation as the other man walked into he room with her.

"Where's Theo?" she asked, and Ellington James nodded his head toward the man that had escorted her into the room. He immediately walked out and closed the door behind him. She heard it lock.

"Sweet, sweet woman, it doesn't matter where Theo is. The point is that he gave me permission to spend some time with you. That is what I am planning to do." He looked her body over from a few feet away. She didn't like his fake accent and couldn't tell if he was trying to be British or Australian. His designer tux said a lot about him as well as the arrogance in his eyes and his stance. She turned to look toward the doorway.

"No need to worry. We're all alone. Let's discuss what's going to happen, shall we?" Ellington approached swiftly, and in no time at all he had ahold of her wrist.

She tried to pull away.

"Don't touch me. I don't know who you think you are, but you have no right to touch me."

She pulled from his hold and ran toward the door. Turning the knob, she knew it was locked. As she turned, Ellington pressed her hard against the door.

"You are the most beautiful of Freda's escorts. You're new, fresh, and the top desire of many men in this circle." He shoved harder, plastering her body against the door as he pressed his mouth against her neck.

"Get off of me," she yelled as she tried to push him away.

"Not going to happen. Just give in, like the others, and I promise I'll pay you well."

Mariana was so angry and disgusted she became enraged at his insult. She wasn't a whore. What had this man done to other women? Did Freda know? Mariana panicked as she began to fight against his restraint. He shoved her head hard against the door nearly stunning her. She retaliated back by slamming her head against his face, surprising him a moment as he released her. She pressed the button hard on her dress then attempted to swing at Ellington. He caught her fist and grabbed her face hard. She screamed and swung her arms until he knocked her onto the rug. He was pulling at her dress, ripping the material as she scratched at his face, his eyes until he hit her. The hit shocked her and hurt so bad she began to cry. His hands were everywhere, groping, pressing until suddenly the door burst open. Ellington was straddling her at the time, and she instantly saw Jax and Jameson.

"You bastard. Get away from her." Jax pulled Ellington up and off of her. More people entered the room, and it was total chaos. She could hear Jax telling his brother to calm down or he was going to kill the man.

Then Jameson was kneeling beside her.

"Jesus, Mariana," he whispered, with intensity in his eyes and fear. He pulled her up into his arms and cradled her on his lap as she cried.

"It's over, baby. He can't hurt you now."

She wouldn't look around to see the crowd of people that gathered. She clung to Jameson, finding safety in his arms and the fact that he was so big and strong.

"Is she okay? Should we call an ambulance?" someone asked.

"I think she's just shaken up. The police are on their way. Let me just calm her down first and then we'll look her over," Jameson said as he held her snuggly against his chest.

"I want to go home," she whispered as she wiped the tears from her eyes.

"Is she okay?" *Jax.* She heard his voice and cringed at the tone and intensity.

"Did he?"

"No. We got to her in time. Thank God you realized she was gone and went looking," Jameson said.

"Thank God she hit that button. Fuck," Jax stated, and she slowly pulled away from Jameson's chest to look at both men. Their eyes widened and they were upset.

"I think we need some ice," Theo said from behind Jameson. Jameson reached to her jaw and gently turned her face.

"Does it hurt really badly?"

She nodded her head. The stinging in her jaw wasn't from pressing her face so hard against Jameson's chest. It was from the grip that Ellington had on her face.

She was totally embarrassed as the police arrived and Theo cleared the room of any nosey onlookers. She assumed that Ellington was arrested on the spot and pulled from the room. He was nowhere to be found. Nothing like this ever happened to her before. As she realized she still clung to Jameson, she got ahold of her emotions and started to move out of his embrace. He didn't look happy about it at all.

* * * *

Jameson was trying his hardest to rein in his anger at the situation. Thank God they had gotten to Mariana in time and Jax stopped Ellington James from hurting her further. Now, with Mariana in his arms, it seemed to calm his temper, but he couldn't say the same for his brother Jax. Jax was pacing after Theo and three other men helped to pull him off of Ellington. He was giving the piece of crap a good ass kicking as he deserved. How dare Ellington think he could touch Mariana, or any woman for that matter. Jameson had no tolerance whatsoever for abusive behavior against women.

He felt Mariana begin to ease off of his lap and out of his arms. Her dress was ripped, and he immediately pulled off his jacket and wrapped it around her.

"Are you hurt anywhere else?"

She shook her head and pulled the jacket tightly against her chest. He kept an arm around her waist, but she was stepping back and away from him. He couldn't help the feeling of insult and upset at her move. Did she think that he would hurt her? Was she just frightened still after what happened?

"Mariana, we need to look you over. The police have arrived," Theo interrupted, and Jameson held her gaze. Those large hazel eyes were glossy with tears. Her beautiful face was red and would probably bruise where that asshole hurt her. The fury must have reached his eyes, because Mariana's hazel ones widened and she quickly moved with Theo toward the officers.

"Is she okay?" Jax asked in rushed words.

"I think so. We got to her quickly enough."

"What took her so long to hit the fucking button?" Jax asked, and he sounded annoyed at Mariana.

"Hey, she was in a bad situation. Maybe the opportunity wasn't immediately there."

"Or she thinks she can take care of herself, knew that we were her security tonight, and hesitated," Jax said, and Jameson knew that Jax would confront Mariana on this. He just hoped he waited long enough for them to be alone.

They stood side by side and watched as the two officers spoke with her. One looked seasoned and the other kind of young, and both seemed overly interested and sensitive to Mariana. Jameson looked at Jax, and he appeared to be thinking the same thing. Jax rolled his eyes as the older officer patted her hand and gave it a squeeze. Both Jameson and Jax clenched their teeth when the young cop placed his fingers under her chin and looked at the red, almost bruised appearance of her cheek. Jameson was about to demand that they stop touching her. She was their woman, their responsibility. When the two cops finally finished up taking down her information and ensuring that a trip to the hospital wasn't necessary, everyone else began to clear the room. It was now just Theo, Mariana, Jameson, and Jax.

"I'll escort you home, Mariana," Theo said, and Jax, Jameson, and Mariana all replied in synch with a "no."

Theo widened his eyes.

"She is after all, my date this evening. I was supposed to drive her back to Freda's place."

"We'll take care of it," Jax said firmly and with a bit of attitude.

Theo raised his eyes, looked Jax and him over before turning to Mariana, who still clung to Jameson's jacket.

"Are you certain about this? I feel responsible for leaving you and allowing you out of my sight," Theo said as he stepped closer to Mariana. She lowered her eyes as Theo cupped her chin and tilted it up toward him.

"Is it okay that Jax and Jameson bring you to Freda's?"

She glanced at Jameson and Jax, and she looked like she got the message that she'd better say yes. They were her security among other things, and she needed to trust them to keep her safe.

"Yes," she whispered.

"I hope to see you again, Mariana. Perhaps I'll contact you?"

She smiled, and that pissed Jameson off big-time.

No, she won't be calling you. She's ours.

He kissed her on the cheek and walked out of the room.

"I can call Benny or Alvin. My purse is here," she said as she reached for her black clutch that sat on the rug by the table.

"No need to. We let Benny go, over an hour ago," Jax replied. He stared at Mariana, and she immediately noticed it.

"Then I'll call a cab," she said as she began to walk. Jax stepped in front of her and gently held her in place by her hips. She stared up into his eyes as Jameson moved closer, too.

She was looking between both of them. From where Jameson stood, he knew she was intimidated. Anyone in their right mind would be. He and his brother were tall and big men. They both believed they carried themselves well, and right now Jax was still on alert and in security mode.

"We will escort you to Freda's. She is waiting on you. You'll change and then we'll bring you home."

Her lips parted, as she was about to object when he pulled her against his chest.

He had trouble catching his breath.

"I've never been so scared," Jax whispered over the top of her head.

"Neither have I," she replied softly, then looked up into Jax's eyes. He brushed his thumb across her bottom lip.

"Why don't we skip Freda's, tell her you're okay, and bring you back to our place? There's things for us to discuss and now is as good a time as any."

Jameson held his breath, waiting for her decline but was shocked when she held Jax's gaze and whispered a soft "okay."

Chapter 8

Mariana didn't know why she said okay to Jax's suggestion or demand or whatever it was. He looked so angry, and so did Jameson, that she should be fearful, but instead, she had that burning in her belly. It was so crazy. She was attacked, and it could have been worse if both men hadn't come to her rescue or if she hadn't hit that safety button. She shivered at the thoughts.

Stealing a glance at both men, she thought they were incredibly good looking. They seemed to care, but there was also this underlying control in their tones of voices and the way they did things. It was a dominance, and beyond just boss or leader aura. It both intimidated her and turned her on. Her body was a sure giveaway to the attraction of that control they seemed to emit.

Yet, they also seemed to care about her. Was it foolish for her to want that, to want someone, or two, to care about her safety? Perhaps she was reading into her reasoning too much. Sure, she was afraid for them to see where she lived, so going back to her place was a huge no. Then she didn't want Freda to see her injuries. The poor woman would be so displeased, and she didn't want to cause Freda any heartache. She had done so much for her.

"Come with us," Jax whispered then wrapped an arm around her shoulders. They exited through a back door, and she was grateful. She really didn't want the guests to see her. Not with her ripped dress and all.

She was oversensitive to everything happening. She was in tune to the darkness of the night as both men flanked either side of her body and whisked her off into the night. All the guests were still inside the estate. She would be completely alone with them shortly. The thought made her body tighten, and her nipples felt so oversensitive and hard, and this turned her on. She was definitely sexually attracted to these two strong, wealthy and resourceful men. As they walked, she would feel one of their thighs brush against her hip, and it felt like a sting of warmth and something more radiated through her skin.

She heard Jameson speaking into his cell phone as they headed across the walkway and into another clearing behind the house. Finally they approached an area where cars and limos were parked. She heard Jameson, and he was speaking to Freda. He kept repeating that Mariana was okay and that they were taking care of her. Her belly did a series of somersaults as Jax stopped next to a Range Rover.

She was going to reach for the handle on the back door, but Jax opened the front passenger door for her to get in. She did and he closed the door as Jax got into the driver side and Jameson hopped into the backseat.

"Freda said she will call you tomorrow. She asked if you needed anything, to please call her." Jameson sounded as though he was speaking through clenched teeth, but it was dark and she couldn't see his face.

As Jax pulled out of the parking lot and onto the highway, she began to question her decision. Why expose herself to more disappointment tonight? Even if something wonderful happened between her, Jax, and Jameson, it would change the moment reality arrived on the scene. In her case, it would be when she got back to her apartment.

She closed her eyes and only jerked a moment when Jax took her hand into his own and squeezed. His reassurance did more than just quicken her heart rate. She had never been so in tune to two people in her life. Their masculinity encompassed the inside of the vehicle. She closed her eyes and allowed the scent to caress her body with each inhale of breath she took. She pulled the lapel of the tuxedo jacket closer to her face. It smelled like Jameson. She clutched it tightly with her free hand. It aroused her entirely too much to know that Jameson sat quietly in the seat directly behind her and that Jax stared straight ahead, determined to get home instead of bothering to force a conversation based on nonsense.

She could be making a huge mistake right now, but her body was overruling her mind. She had always been a pessimist and allowed bad thoughts to rule her actions. Not now. Not tonight. Something amazing happened between her and Jax earlier in the evening. His kiss lingered in the back of her mind. Then, as Jameson embraced her and offered her his coat, she felt that spark of respect, acknowledgement of sincere care, and it egged her on to take a chance at what they offered. Whatever it was. No matter how bizarre.

Of course as the car rolled to a stop, she blinked open her eyes in time to realize that the men lived in one of that largest, most elite apartment buildings in Houston.

She swallowed hard as Jax parked the car and she pulled her hand away and clutched the jacket.

Jameson opened her door and escorted her out of the underground parking area, set aside for penthouse-suite residents. At least that was what the sign indicated both before the entryway and now that they were inside.

She should have figured as much.

They were still silent, but now Jameson took her hand and gave it a squeeze.

"Are you cold, baby?" he asked in a low, sexy tone. How could four simple words send sexual fire against her chest and straight into her pussy? She nodded, and he pulled her closer against his side. Her clit actually throbbed. Was that even possible? She had never been this in tune to her body before and especially her sexual organ. With every step, her pussy swelled as the friction between her thighs even aroused her oversensitive body. She felt her insecurities begin to overwhelm her. But what were the choices now, if not this? She could make them bring her home, to her place? That thought made her feel so insignificant and so out of their league. Two men with such charisma, wealth, and power would find her choice of dwelling a turn-off. Not that it was her choice, but it was where she lived. Freda knew, and Benny and Alvin, and they didn't treat her any differently. They entered the private elevator.

She almost felt like crying. How had her life taken such a turn for worse instead of better? She had been struggling for years to achieve her degree and it was just a damn bachelors degree. It wasn't like med school or a doctorate for crying out loud.

She wiped her eyes before the tear could fall. A glance at Jax and he still had that determined, CEO kind of expression. He was in charge. He had a plan. And then he pressed a key into a special area on the elevator panel. A few seconds later, the doors opened right into an elaborate entryway and formal living room.

"Please, come in and welcome to our home," Jameson said as he led her in. Jax pulled the key from the panel and then the doors closed. He tossed those keys into a hunter-green marble bowl on top of a marble side table. She stood in complete awe. The place was ginormous. She wouldn't even be able to pay for the bowl he tossed his keys into. Her shoulders slumped, and she clutched the tux tighter.

"This is where you live?" she asked, as her heels clicked on the marble flooring and Jameson led her further into the room. Thank God she wore the designer dress. At least in the clothing she felt closer to their level. *Yeah, keep telling yourself that, Sparks.*

Jax disappeared a moment as Jameson showed her around. These men were rich. They were wealthier than she imagined. She realized as she passed the modern kitchen, filled with stainless steel appliances and other appliances and contraptions, she had no idea what they were. But she did know that the kitchen was bigger than her entire apartment. That was another dose of reality.

He led her to another room as they passed the Houston skyline and windows that stretched from floor to practically ceiling. They were high up, and the view at night was gorgeous.

He stopped at another room where the view continued to take her breath away. Jax was there. He was fixing snifters of brandy and he downed one rather quickly. She paused where she was, concerned that he might get drunk or something.

"Jax?" she whispered, and he gripped the bar as if in deep thought.

Jameson began to take the jacket off of her shoulders. She was glad that the dress wasn't ripped up top and only below.

"I need a moment, Mariana."

She felt Jameson's hands on her shoulders as he caressed her arms. She tried to look around the room, and then she spotted it. The painting from the gallery. Jack Vettriano's *Lovers and Other Strangers*. She swallowed hard.

Jax followed her line of sight. She absorbed the structure of his face, the determined, muscular image he portrayed right now as he removed his tuxedo jacket. Dressed in all black, it made him appear mysterious, provocative and damn sexy. Every bit of her body was in tune to him as well as Jameson.

"I told you, it was one of my favorites," Jax whispered, holding her gaze.

Jameson caressed a hand down her waist, across her hip, then to her belly. She closed her eyes and absorbed the feel of him and his actions like that in the painting. If she wanted them, she could have them. She could live for tonight, in this moment, and worry about reality tomorrow. This could be a fantasy come true. As a lover of art and the emotion it inspired, she felt herself ease into Jameson's touch and await their guidance. Thoughts that these two fine men did things like this often only flashed into her mind. What did she have to offer them? Her body, perhaps her soul, because of the weak-minded fool she was? Why waste time and concern over the unknown when the present actions took precedence over all other thoughts?

She felt Jameson's lips against the back of her neck. Tiny goose bumps scattered underneath her skin as her arms fell to her sides, a sure sign of her compliance and acceptance. His large, thick hand was pressed against her belly, and he used the knuckles of his other hand to glide up and down her back, against the fabric of the dress.

"You are so beautiful, Mariana. I've never been this attracted to a woman before. You make me want things," he whispered then moved those kisses along her shoulder. His whiskers tickled her skin and burned her flesh. That stinging lit a spark of some sort, and all she could do was focus on her rapid breathing and Jameson's. Then she sensed Jax directly in front of her. She inhaled deeply. His cologne filled her senses along with his masculinity. He was built well and solid. Even with eyes closed she could sense it.

She opened her eyes, could feel how glazed over they were. He appeared even larger in this enclosed space. Her nipples hardened to tiny buds, and she inhaled a shaky breath.

"Stay here with us tonight. Let us make love to you, Mariana. We need you desperately," Jameson said as he began to lower the zipper on the back of her dress.

Immediately the material fell from her body, pooled to the floor, and Jax's eyes widened then darkened. She wore a strapless bra and very skimpy thin thong panties with garters. The dress was very fitted and she didn't want panty lines to show.

Jax licked his lips.

"Gorgeous."

"Perfect," Jameson said as Jax's hand caressed over her ass then back toward the front of her body.

Jax stepped closer, cupped her face gently between his hands as he stared down into her eyes.

"Tonight you're ours. Don't think about tomorrow or anything that occurred earlier. Let us love you, Mariana."

Her heart soared with excitement and desire. She was utterly turned on, and when Jax's lips touched her own, she couldn't resist touching him back.

She clung to him as he devoured her moans and explored her mouth. She felt Jameson's hand move down her body pressing the panties out of the way then finding her clit.

She jerked, and Jax kissed her harder while Jameson pressed deeper. He parted her pussy lips with thumb and finger then pressed upward. She parted her thighs, and lifted one leg slowly up against Jax's thigh to give Jameson better access to her body. She was on fire.

* * * *

Jax felt like some wild animal desperate to mate. Mariana was incredible. Her skin soft and her body firm. The undergarments she wore barely covered the parts he wanted to claim next. He pulled slowly from her lips and breathed heavily against her mouth. She panted in sync.

"Are you on the pill?" he asked, and her eyes widened as she shook her head.

Jameson kissed along her neck as he continued to stroke Mariana's pussy.

"We'll take care of everything," Jameson whispered.

Jax began to remove his clothing as he kept his eyes locked with Mariana's.

"Hold on to the arms of that recliner and bend over," Jameson ordered, and she did.

Jax watched in admiration as her milky thighs parted, black garters and all, and she bent over with her beautiful ass pointed at Jameson.

His brother smiled as he caressed the globes then reached under to stroke her cunt.

Her lips parted, her head hung low, and her hands gripped the arms of the chair.

"That's it, baby, just like that," Jax whispered, removing all his clothes.

"She's so wet for us, Jax. Our woman wants to make love," Jameson said as he stroked his fingers in and out of her pussy from behind.

"Is that right, baby? Do you want us tonight?" Jax asked as he gently pushed the strands of hair from her face, making her turn toward him. His heart pounded at the sight of her expression. Sexuality, innocence, desire all ready for him to take. She licked her lips, and his cock hardened and tapped against his belly.

"You got my cock nice and hard, Mariana. I can't wait to be inside of you."

"Yes, oh please, Jax, I feel so—"

Jameson increased the speed of his finger thrusts, making her lose her breath as the first orgasm hit her.

"Let it go. Just feel it and release it. We want all your orgasms tonight," Jameson said, and she moaned then thrust her ass back against Jameson.

Jax couldn't resist touching her as he ran the palm of his hand across her ass and squeezed.

He whispered next to her ear.

"I'm going to fuck your pussy so hard, baby, while Jameson fucks this beautiful round ass."

"Oh!" Mariana moaned louder, and he could feel her body shaking.

"Let's do it, Jax. I won't be able to hold off."

"I hear you."

Jax immediately ripped open the foil and placed the condom on. He kissed Mariana then maneuvered into the recliner.

Jameson pulled his fingers from her pussy and she gasped as she immediately grabbed onto Jax's shoulders.

"Get rid of the bra. I want to see what belongs to me."

Jameson unclipped it and pulled it from her body. Her breasts were big and more than a handful. He cupped them with both hands as she tilted her head back. Over her shoulder, Jax could see Jameson undressing.

"You ready for us, baby?"

He pulled her toward him and sucked on her breasts, nipping the nipple before swirling his tongue around the areola. As she panted and thrust her pussy over his cock, he licked the other breast, getting her ready for him.

"I want in now."

"Yes," she replied.

"Then do it. Take my cock into your hands and claim me, woman," he stated firmly, and he saw the flash of excitement and shock in her eyes. His cock jerked.

As Mariana's fingers touched his penis, he squeezed her breasts.

"Faster, baby, I want to be inside of you when I come."

She lowered herself onto his cock and slowly sank down on him. But he couldn't take it. She was so fucking tight.

"Fuck, baby, you're killing me."

"Let me help," Jameson said as he pressed her shoulders gently downward then parted her ass cheeks. She sank fully onto Jax's cock, and they both moaned.

"Fucking beautiful," Jameson whispered.

Jax grabbed hold of her hips and began to thrust upward, helping her to move. She moaned and whimpered, making him hungrier and even more aroused.

"Those fucking sweet sounds she makes. I love it." He shoved upward, and then she began to join him. She was moving her hips, stroking his cock relentlessly.

"Slow down, baby, Jameson is joining us," he said, and she paused a moment and he knew she needed guidance.

"Ever have a cock in your ass, sugar?" Jameson asked, and she froze and her body tightened.

"I think not, Jameson. Go slowly," Jax said.

"Of course. Trust me, Mariana. I won't hurt you and I promise that this is going to feel so good. I've wanted you since the first time I saw you." He kissed along her neck, and she reached up and touched his cheek. Jameson kissed her palm then pulled her finger into his mouth and sucked the digit.

Her expressions were priceless. Jax thought she was too good to be real. She was innocent, sexy, and all woman.

"Relax, and ride Jax while I get this sexy ass ready for me."

She did as Jameson said and she lifted up and down onto Jax's cock. Jax held her hips until Jameson indicated that he was getting the lube and preparing to insert it.

Jax wrapped his arms around her and held her to his chest.

"Oh God. Oh," she moaned as Jameson worked the lube into her ass.

"Such a pretty, tight, pink hole. Your ass is sucking in my fingers, baby."

Her body shook as she lifted then thrust backward against Jameson's fingers and onto Jax's cock.

"Oh yeah. A natural. Come on, Jameson. Lets claim what's ours," Jax whispered then held her tight.

* * * *

Jameson felt harder than a steel rod. He knew he wasn't going to last long at all. Mariana was too damn sexy and appealing. From her beautiful hazel eyes, to her sexy curvy body, she was everything he ever wanted in a woman. Her ass was perfect, too, and as he eased his cock slowly through the tight rings, he heard her whimpers and moans and couldn't take it.

"Baby, I wish you could see this. You're pulling my cock in deeper and deeper. Tell me how badly you want me in your ass. Please, baby."

"Move, oh God, it burns and I feel full and, oh!" She moaned, and he felt her body release another orgasm and ease up enough for him to shove inward. He grabbed hold of her hips and slowly thrust in and out of her ass.

"That's it, baby, so beautiful," Jax whispered as he cupped her cheeks and stared into her eyes.

"You're ours, Mariana. All ours," Jameson said and then he and Jax began to thrust in and out of her in sync.

"I can't hold back. Too fucking tight," Jameson said then thrust hard into her.

She screamed then pushed downward onto Jax's cock, and he exploded next as he latched his mouth onto her breast. She thrust again and again trying to find her release and then exploded as she moaned and swayed.

"Oh damn, Mariana, that was amazing," Jax told her, and then held her tightly against his chest.

Jameson caressed her back, massaging her skin as he laid kisses along her shoulder.

"I'm going to pull out nice and slowly, baby. You're so amazing," he said then gently pulled from her ass.

He walked away to grab a washcloth, and when he returned, Mariana and Jax were still embraced, his cock still deep within her. He smiled wide. This was what they dreamed about for years. This was what locked them together now forever.

"I'll wash you up, love," Jameson said, and Jax slowly lifted her up then turned her around to face Jameson. The sight of her large round breasts and blotchy fair skin aroused him all over again. Jax spread her thighs, and she tried to pull them together.

"Don't. This is ours," he said as he trailed his finger slowly down her pussy then lower. She gasped and tightened up.

"You are ours, and we're going to take care of you." Jameson reached down and began to clean her and then picked her up into his arms to carry her to their bed.

* * * *

Mariana didn't know how she was still breathing, never mind lusting over Jameson and Jax. Their bodies were perfection. Jax had laid her down onto a very large bed. King-size, with a thick, soft white comforter. She could sleep for hours in such a bed. That thought made her chest tighten. This wasn't anything more than lust. The three of them were so sexually charged that having sex was bound to happen. So why was she feeling sad and rejected at the thought of giving so much to two strangers and getting nothing but her lonely life in return? Was it regrets? Was she latching on to something that wasn't there?

Shit, Mariana. Why hadn't you thought this through before you let them both take you? Oh Lord, I had sex with two men. I had anal sex! Oh God, what have I done?

"You're not leaving, so get any crazy ideas you have out of your head," Jameson stated firmly. She swallowed hard as she lay on her side and tried covering her breasts. What did it matter with her ass sticking out as Jax joined them on the bed?

She stared up at Jameson and the scowl on his face. His cock was thick and big even in sleeping stage. She noticed the faded scar along his waist and the dips and curves of his body to his chest muscles.

He reached over and cupped her chin with thumb and pointer. "We should ice this some more." His voice sounded hard.

"I have some right here," Jax said, making her turn quickly toward him.

"Oh God," she said aloud, and Jax smirked as he climbed onto the bed, wearing only a pair of boxers. He was exquisite. With large wide shoulders, long, solid, muscular arms, and a trim waist. Even his legs were muscular.

Jameson rolled her to her back, Jax placed the ice against her cheek, and she tried to roll over to cover her breasts and pussy, but both men stopped her.

"No need to be shy. You're going to be spending a lot of time naked and in this bed. Get used to it," Jax remarked, and she felt her cheeks warm and a mix of emotions fill her. He was bossy and demanding. He got what he wanted when he wanted it. She should run for her life, but foolish her was turned on by his tone and of course his incredible body. *I'm an idiot.*

"We're going to be spending a lot of time together," Jax said then gently caressed his hand over her belly. She tensed up as she stared into his eyes.

"Don't talk like that. I get what this is. I accepted it. Please don't sugarcoat it."

Jax lifted the ice from her cheek.

"Sugarcoat it?" he repeated, and she nodded her head.

Jameson climbed between her thighs and knelt above her. She stared up into his dark-blue eyes and wondered what he was going to do or demand.

"Why didn't you press the panic button earlier?"

She was not expecting that question, and as she lowered her eyes and began to turn away Jax raised his voice.

"Answer him."

She looked at Jax. He was so damn serious. She should feel intimidated and concerned for her well-being. So why was every feminine part of her body aroused and growing wet?

"I don't know," she whispered, and Jameson pushed down on the bed with his fists making the bed dip slightly. Her breasts bounced from the abrupt movement.

"Why?"

"I don't know, Jameson. I didn't think that it would get that far. I didn't want to think that I could be a victim to a man's sexual assault."

"He could have raped you," Jax added, and the tears hit her eyes at the realization of how close she had come to that fate.

"I'm sorry I don't have a better answer for you than the truth. I'm used to handling things on my own. I don't have anyone to do it for me. It was me and him," she admitted as the feelings of how alone in the world she truly was hit home hard. The tears welled up in her eyes.

"You're wrong," Jax stated then reached across and touched a finger to her nipple. She felt the shot of fire run through her breast and straight to her pussy as he stroked that nipple and continued to arouse her. A tear escaped from her eye. She shouldn't show weakness with men like these two. She knew nothing about them or their intentions. Things were running amuck rather quickly.

"You're not alone anymore. You have us," Jameson said, and she felt the tip of his cock against her folds. She sucked in a deep breath as she held his gaze.

"I don't think you get what's happened here tonight. You really think that this is a game? That we would bring you to our home, fuck you, then make you leave in the morning?" Jameson asked as he reached down and stroked her pussy with the tip of his cock. She burned with need. She wanted this to mean so much more, but he was confusing her.

She turned her head slowly side to side in disbelief.

"Please, Jameson, I don't know what you want from me. This is not normal for me. The last two weeks have been unexpected."

He pressed the tip of his cock between her folds. She felt her pussy grip the bulbous bit of flesh, and it wanted more. She thrust her hips slowly forward in an attempt to get him all the way inside of her.

"We know you're not easy. That's not the concern. The concern is the fact that Jax told you that we were there tonight as your security.

You were informed about how and when to use that button. Yet, you failed to do it quickly enough."

"And it nearly cost you. I nearly killed that man for attempting to hurt you," Jax added and then cupped her breast.

"Why are you both so angry?" she asked, and Jameson pressed his cock deeper into her.

She parted her lips and held on to his forearms. Her body welcomed his invasion.

"You belong to us and we care about you. That scene, that moment of knowing you were in trouble and breaking down the door to see him on top of you, enraged me," Jameson said as he held himself within her.

Her eyes widened as a feeling of belonging, being wanted tried to squeeze its way into her hardened heart.

She fought it tooth and nail even though the sensation of his thick hard cock sitting still inside of her made her shake with need for him to move and to fuck her.

"It won't happen again. I'm sorry I made your job difficult."

Jameson pulled out then shoved back in hard, making her gasp but arousing her more. She felt her pussy clench and leak. Oh God, he was so forceful and sexy when he was angry.

"You're right it won't happen again," Jameson stated firmly as he stroked in and out of her pussy.

Mariana tried to calm her excitement at his control. *What's wrong with me? I'm turned on entirely too much by his aggression.*

He lifted up, pulled nearly all the way out, then thrust into her harder, deeper. This time she ran the palms of her hands up his chest and pulled him firmer to her. He kissed her hard on the mouth, and she opened to his assault. She parted her thighs wider, wanting his cock to reach her womb and bring her the satisfaction she needed after the ache he caused.

He moved his lips off of her mouth and toward her neck. He continued to thrust in and out of her as she dug her heels into his ass cheeks trying to get him deeper.

"More, Jameson, more," she yelled, and he slowed down and paused inside of her. He looked down into her eyes, and she wanted to scream for him to continue. It felt so damn good.

"I want you to trust me, Mariana. Trust that I'll take care of you and so will Jax."

What was he saying? Why such seriousness?

"I don't want to think about anything else right now, Jameson. I just want you both to make love to me. All this intensity is making me crazy with confusion," she said then tried to pull from him. In a flash he lifted her up from the bed with one arm around her waist, and as she wondered what he was doing, she saw Jax. He was standing by the bed, placing a condom on his cock. Jameson flipped her around, stunning her at his agility and strength to move her around like a rag doll.

He was on his back, about to lie down when Jax lifted her up from around her waist and she watched Jameson put on the condom.

"You want us to just make love to you and save the talk for later? Then that's what we'll do," Jameson said as he grabbed hold of her hips and impaled her onto his cock. She moaned at the sensation of instant fullness and then after two upward pumps from Jameson, she felt Jax's hands pressing her back downward so that her chest touched Jameson's. Her heart pounded in her chest, and her puckered hole felt as if it responded to the indication of what was coming. She craved it and she couldn't help but wiggle her ass.

Smack.

"Hey."

The smack came out of nowhere.

"Watch where you're wiggling that, baby. Jameson took it easy on you before. I'm a bit different when it comes to fucking my woman's ass."

"Oh God, please, Jax. Please go slowly," she begged. She shivered from his words, the deep tone of his voice, and of course the fact that he referred to her as his woman. She could only dream such a fairy tale would come true.

He ran his hand up her spine and took hold of her hair. She felt the chills run over her flesh as her breasts pushed forward and her lips parted.

"You're done being an escort. There's nothing to discuss." He covered her lips with his own and kissed her quickly on the mouth just as his words sunk in. She wanted to protest to say what gave him the right, but he chose that moment to part her ass cheeks and press some lube to her anus. Jameson thrust upward and held her neck and cheek in his large hand.

"Come down here and kiss me. I love the way you taste," Jameson said and drew her in for a heavy kiss. A moment later, as his tongue stroked her mouth, Jax pressed his cock through the tight rings and thrust balls deep. Pulling from Jameson's mouth she moaned as the burning and full sensation filled her.

"Oh God, I can't take it."

"You will take it," Jameson said then thrust upward.

"Escorting job is finished. Understood," Jax said then began to stroke into her ass as Jameson counterthrust into her pussy. She was on a roller coaster of emotions. They wanted her. They were so big and hard and sexy, why not allow them to control her? Then came the fears of being hurt and disappointed. It was the cycle of her life. But with every stroke, with every endearment of passion and desire that left their lips or encased her with their bodies and hands, she relinquished her hold on independence. It ultimately led her to believe that happiness could be reached. The questions was, could she give up that control completely and allow two men to care for her while she let go of her past and all its mistakes?

Chapter 9

"So things didn't go quite as planned," Buster told Clover as he joined him outside of the Centurion Estate.

"Why not? It was simple enough and Ellington is a pro at what he does. There's not a slimier womanizer in existence."

"Yeah, well, Mariana had bodyguards. Jax and Jameson Spaulding."

Clover squinted his eyes and tried to stand straight without swaying. He was a bit drunk. A precelebration of what was to come.

"That wasn't planned. How far did Ellington go?"

"From what I found out, he was straddling her on the floor, about to force her into submitting."

"Hmmm. That must have been a sight. I knew that Ellington would jump at the opportunity to have Mariana. She is quite stunning and youthful. There's almost a pure innocence about her. Virginal, actually."

"Yeah, well, she disappeared."

"Probably back to Freda's. That woman has taken a major liking to Mariana." Clover began to walk toward his limo and Buster followed.

"What would you like me to do next?"

"Maybe let the rumor start. Let them know that someone is trying to frazzle them and will take anything that is valuable from them. Perhaps a small but direct message that states I'll go as far as I have to for revenge. That should keep them unhappy."

Buster smiled. "I'll take care of that. What about the information on the Spaulding brothers possibly being hired as security for Darian Rothesburgh? The heist you were planning could be compromised."

"X-Caliber hasn't gotten the contract yet. I was schmoozing with Rothesburgh earlier. I put in a good word about Pro Tech Security being the best. As long as he uses them, then the heist will be successful. When Rothesburgh has those one-of-a-kind paintings delivered to the community gallery show next month, they'll disappear. I have men in place and the security will be easy to penetrate with Pro Tech in charge. I had people placed in the security company a year ago in preparation for this event. How stupid of Rothesburgh to even allow such fine and unique pieces to be on display in a community center hotel. We got this. We'll work it out. Just send the message."

Clover smiled as he got into his limo and left the estate.

* * * *

Mariana got out of the shower and found a thick, fluffy, black robe sitting folded on the bathroom vanity. She was completely in awe of the bathroom in the penthouse and the huge walk-in shower with way too many showerheads. Jameson had a remote control that set the direction of each head plus the temperature, too. When she asked about the contraption, he shrugged his shoulders as he mumbled something about him creating it. Jax chimed in about Jameson being humble and that he was some kind of inventor. The thought made her feel a mix of emotions. She was proud of him, which was odd, because that was a silly feeling to have for a man she hardly knew and whom was much older than her. She felt intimidated, once again, as thoughts of not being good enough for Jax and Jameson entered her mind. Finally, she felt sad about leaving them, and leaving them was a definite must so that she couldn't get hurt. This situation wasn't real. It couldn't be real. Every time she glanced around their penthouse and absorbed all the decorations, the items, she could never afford, she reminded herself about her apartment. That small closet of a space was all she had. It would never be a home. It would never provide safety and warmth like their penthouse instantly made her feel. Safe. Here in this place, with Jax and Jameson, she felt safe. She didn't think she was a scared or timid individual, so why now? Why, when being exposed to a different way of life, did she feel so minuscule and in need of reassurances?

As she placed the robe on, she dried her hair and thought about how weak Jameson and Jax made her and the power they already held over her. Just thinking about their bodies and their good looks made her feel wanton and needy. But when she thought about beyond last night and this morning, she couldn't see herself being truly loved by them or cherished. She just didn't think she had anything to offer them. They were at least ten years older than her. They served in the military and experienced war. They established themselves in a lucrative career and were extremely wealthy. Jameson was an inventor. *An inventor! I'm not even finished with college. I live in a shitty neighborhood and piece-of-crap, one-bedroom apartment and I have bills, bills, and more bills. This isn't going to work. I'm not good enough for them.*

* * * *

Jameson was whistling as he cooked up the bacon and eggs. Jax sat in the chair at the table dressed for the day in dark dress pants and a dark-burgundy shirt.

"We need to make some changes right away," Jax stated.

Jameson turned toward his brother as he pulled the last pieces of bacon from the pan then turned off the burner.

"What changes are you referring to?"

"We need her here with us. We should have her things brought here, the last month's rent paid so she can leave and move her in here immediately." Jax pulled out his phone. "I can have everything done within the next few hours."

"Whoa. Hold on a minute. I think Mariana is going to have something to say about this, Jax."

Jax tried to calm his breathing.

"She was almost raped, Jameson. Men look at her and want her. She's ours," he said so firmly and with such conviction he even shocked himself. He was acting like an animal, an alpha male staking his claim.

Jameson ran his fingers through his damp hair.

"Listen, I feel exactly how you feel, but Mariana is scared. For Christ's sake, Jax, she didn't hit the panic button right away even knowing that we were there for her. She's used to being alone, dealing with things on her own and with no help. If we come into this relationship and smother her, we'll just be pushing her away. We need to ease into this. This is the real deal for me. Marriage, a family, and maybe spending more time in the country. She's been on her own and she needs reassurance from us."

"I don't like it. Let's cut out the bullshit and just tell her this is the way it is."

Jameson shook his head.

"No. Trust me on this one. She'll bolt. I already think she wants to leave now."

Jax stood up.

"Leave? She's not leaving and going back to that neighborhood. Something might happen to her. She's staying here and that is final."

"Jax?"

They turned to see Mariana standing in the open foyer from the hallway where the bedrooms were.

She had her arms wrapped around her waist and the robe was way too big for her small frame.

"Good morning, baby. Breakfast is ready. How was the shower?" Jameson asked as he swiftly made his way toward Mariana. Jax thought she looked gorgeous and so petite standing there in the huge black robe. He could wake up to seeing her like this every morning for the rest of his life. The feelings struck him hard as he quickly turned away from her.

* * * *

Mariana didn't know what was going on, but by the sound of their muffled voices, Jax and Jameson were having a heated argument. It just validated her thoughts that it was time to leave.

Jameson pulled out a chair for her to sit, and then he placed some eggs and bacon onto the plates.

They all sat at the island in the kitchen and quietly ate. She just picked at the bacon and eggs. Normally she would be in heaven eating a breakfast like this. She hadn't had time to hit the store this week and she was surviving on yogurt and peanut butter sandwiches, minus the bread. Her stomach rumbled, and despite her fear of their response when she told Jameson and Jax that she needed to head home, she ate.

"I guess you like my eggs," Jameson said, and when she looked up, both men were watching her.

She felt embarrassed as she wiped her mouth then took a sip of juice.

"They're good."

"When was the last time you ate?" Jax asked with a tone that made her belly quiver and her nipples harden. He was so damn forceful all the time.

She was scared to answer him. Jameson placed a hand on her knee, and she jumped then looked at him.

"When?" Jameson asked.

She cleared her throat. "Last night at the gallery, why?"

Both men exchanged glances.

"What did you have?" Jax asked.

"Why?" she replied.

"What did you have?" he repeated, and she leaned back in the chair and folded her hands on her lap. A glance at her clean plate and then at Jax and Jameson's full ones indicated that she obviously had been eating very quickly and they noticed.

"I had some hors d'oeuvres."

"You must have been starving, by the way you just swallowed those eggs and bacon. You hardly chewed," Jax said then stood up. He took her empty plate and walked over toward the stove to add more eggs and bacon.

"I don't want more," she said, and she was embarrassed for being caught eating like some starving orphan. That thought instantly caused a pain in her belly.

"Eat up. There's more when you're finished with that."

Jax placed a full plate down in front of her, and a quick glance at Jameson and he looked concerned and upset.

She pushed the plate forward.

"I'm done. I don't want anymore."

"Eat it," Jax ordered. He actually ordered her to eat. Was he fucking kidding?

"No." She stood up.

"I think it's time for me to leave. Can you get me my dress Jameson?" she asked and he just stared at her.

"How often do you eat, Mariana?" Jameson asked.

"Why are you giving me the third degree about my eating habits? I'm sorry I wolfed down the food. I was hungry."

"How often?" Jax asked. She sighed in annoyance and crossed her arms in front of her chest. Standing here in just a robe, she felt so exposed to them. It was as if they could see into her life. She couldn't tell them that she was struggling to make ends meet and that more often than not she went to bed hungry. It was a good day if she got to eat a regular meal. That was another bonus to being an escort. The food spreads were phenomenal at the events she attended. It was the one full meal she could look forward to. It was crazy, but even after one escort job, she looked forward to the food almost as much as she looked forward to viewing some fine art.

"I'm watching my figure," she replied with attitude to their stern expressions.

Jax walked toward her, and she instinctively stepped back. Instead of escaping around the island she walked backward and right between Jameson's spread thighs. He clutched her shoulders, and Jax now stood directly in front of her. She had to tilt her head all the way back to look up into his face. He seemed angry, his blue eyes darker, and it appeared as if he was biting his cheek.

She swallowed hard.

"You don't need to watch your figure," he stated as he undid the knot and pushed her robe open. His eyes widened at her nakedness.

"You're perfect," he said firmly, and her entire body heated up.

She was hot from having an argument with Jax. How the hell did this conversation take a turn to wanting both men inside of her again?

He cupped her face between his hands. His thumb brushed along her chin then lower lip as he looked at her bruised cheek and jaw. He was breathing through his nostrils. Jameson took that moment to push her robe off of her shoulders. It fell to the floor. She was standing there completely naked in front of them.

Jax licked his lips.

"You're not leaving. We have things to discuss and work out. Whether you like it or not, we're going to take care of you." Jameson moved his hands toward the front of her body and cupped her breasts. She gasped just as Jax covered her mouth with his own. She lost all focus but the feel of both men touching, kissing her, and arousing her body. Her nipples hardened and her breasts swelled under Jameson's ministrations.

Jax deepened the kiss, devouring her moans as he ran his hands down her throat in a possessive manner. She felt controlled, possessed by them, and it made her pussy clench and her heart race with mixed emotions.

She felt Jax's hand move down her body to her mound. He cupped her flesh, and Jameson continued to kneed her breasts and pluck her nipples.

She pulled her mouth from Jax's mouth and gasped. "Oh God, this is wild. How can you two do this to me?" she asked as Jax's hand still held her throat, and his thumb gently caressed over her skin there, eliciting more excitement to run rampant through her body. She was sexually aroused in the position as their submissive. With two such dominant men it seemed inevitable. They brought this side out in her.

She felt the thick finger maneuver between her pussy lips. Jax pinched her clit, and she leaned back against Jameson.

"Look at me," Jax demanded, and she immediately complied as she locked gazes with his dark-blue eyes.

"You belong to us now. We take care of what's ours. The sooner you understand that and accept it. The better."

He pressed his finger deeper then began to stroke her already wet pussy.

"Ours, Mariana. All ours," Jameson whispered against her neck before he licked and sucked her skin then bit gently into the muscle by her shoulder and neck. She moaned and felt the gush of cream release.

"I love your responsiveness to our touch, baby. Listen to your body, Sparks. Listen to its acknowledgement that it belongs to Jameson and I," Jax whispered as he increased his strokes.

She opened wider for him and wanted to feel more of his fingers thrust into her. She climbed up onto Jameson's lap. He stretched her thighs over his thighs then parted his. She was completely open to Jax's ministrations.

"This is our pussy, our body, and we'll take care of it, like we're going to take care of you. That means, no starving yourself to look good. You're perfect," Jax said then lowered himself to lick across her pussy from bottom to top.

"Put your arms up and behind my neck," Jameson ordered. Now he was getting bossy.

She did as he told her and reached up and back. She clasped her hands behind his neck and head, causing her breasts to push forward against his hands.

She moaned from the sensations.

"Oh, Jameson, I can't take it. It feels too good," she admitted, and he pulled on her nipples hard. He twisted lightly making her thrust her pussy against Jax's face.

They were controlling her body and her mind. Making her wild for their touch, their attention, and ultimately their cocks.

"Please, Jax, Jameson, I need you inside of me."

Jax swiped a finger from her pussy to her anus then pressed a finger over the puckered hole and through the tight rings. She exploded on the spot.

"Oh!" She moaned loudly and jerked her hips forward as she rode out the orgasm.

"Fuck, Jax, I can't take it. I need inside of her now," Jameson said.

In a flash they were lifting her up and carrying her out of the kitchen. She didn't know what was happening as Jax began to undress then lie down on the long black ottoman. He spread his legs wide and Jameson placed her onto Jax. Jax grabbed her by the waist, and she immediately took him inside of her. Her pussy clenched and spasmed from the invasion of Jax's hard cock. She immediately felt it to her womb and she began to ride him. She felt wild, sexy, and utterly turned on beyond belief. Up and down, back and forth, she rode him fast. But then Jax grabbed her hair and yanked her down toward his chest, shocking her.

She gasped as their noses touched. He looked so wild and out of control.

"You belong to us. I won't let you go. This isn't a one-night stand or a weekend fling. Get that through your head, 'cause things are going to change." Her heart hammered in her chest. She felt the cool liquid to her anus, and then Jameson's cock pushed through the tight rings without warning.

"Oh!" she screamed, and both men began to rock into her. Their fast, deep penetrations caused her to lose her breath. The reality of what these men did to her and made her feel brought tears to her eyes. She loved them. She was such a fool, but she loved them already. She wanted so much from them yet feared being hurt and being left all alone again.

She felt the tears roll down her cheeks, and something carnal and crazy came over her. She began to meet them thrust for thrust. Their bodies became one, and she wasn't certain who was pulling on her nipples, who was gripping her hair, and who was moaning along with her. They united like nothing she had ever felt before. Both cocks stroked her deeply, and just as she thought she could catch a full breath, she gasped from their thrusts. Her body tightened and she screamed her release as both Jameson and Jax roared like wild men as their bodies slapped against hers.

She felt them explode inside of her as she collapsed against Jax's chest.

Their heavy breathing filled the room. No one said a word, and she felt Jax caress the tears from her wet cheeks. He cupped her face and stared into her glossy eyes. He knew she cried. But somehow he knew why and that they hadn't hurt her, but that she felt the connection.

"Incredible. You felt it, didn't you, Mariana?" She nodded her head as more tears escaped her eyes, and Jameson's lips pressed against her shoulders as he gripped her hair. She turned up toward him, her breast no longer against Jax's chest but open to his mouth. He latched onto her nipple as Jameson thrust his cock into her ass as a reminder that she was his possession.

"That feeling we all had? I want that all the time. I want it with you, Mariana."

He kissed her on the mouth, and she relished in the moment and the aftermath of their lovemaking. Deep, in the back of her mind were feelings of reservation, but in this moment the power of their lovemaking overruled any other thoughts or fears. *I love them. God help me, but I love them.*

Chapter 10

"I don't understand what the problem is, Spider. I thought that Darian Rothesburgh wanted to go with our services for that art event. He was greatly concerned over the security of the location and how accessible it is," Jax asked Spider as he sat in the home office while Jameson and Mariana got ready to leave for Freda's estate.

"I know. I think that someone talked him out of using our company for security. I can't help to think that this may have something to do with Clover Masters and the security breach we discussed the other night."

Jax released an annoyed sigh.

"Where have you gotten with the investigation into the computer breach?"

"Nowhere. It's like they caught on to it and disappeared."

"What about the person you thought might be the leak?"

"Her computer was bugged and monitored."

"I should have had a word with Clover last night at the estate. He was there and appeared kind of pompous."

"By the way, I heard about what happened with Mariana. Lucky that you and Jameson were there. Is she okay?"

"She's doing better."

"Making progress?"

"You can say that."

"Watch out for her, Jax. She's special, but she's caught the interest of a lot of people. Including Clover."

"What do you mean?"

"I just have this feeling, you know, that something isn't right. I feel like Clover is out to get you and destroy this company for some reason."

"I don't know what that would have to do with Mariana."

"You and Jameson are staking a claim. That's enough to make Clover want to hurt her. I'm not staying that he had something to do with last night, but he does do business with Ellington James. Ellington has connections to Pro Tech Security."

Jax felt his chest tighten. He was instantly concerned over Mariana's well-being, and suddenly Jameson's plea to go slowly with her was eliminated from thought. He wasn't going to let her live alone at that shit hole apartment.

"I'll take your gut instincts into consideration. Why don't you do Jameson and I a favor and see what you come up with on Ellington and Pro Tech Security. If something doesn't feel right, I'll have a talk with Darian and try to talk him into using our services."

"Sounds good to me. I hate those two assholes and knowing that Ellington touched Mariana is enough for me to rip the guy's fucking throat out if need be."

Jax laughed. "Thanks, Spider. Keep in touch."

Jax hung up the phone and was relieved to have a man like Spider, retired military, on his side. Now, he had to get ready for the fight he was surely going to have with Marian over her moving out of her apartment and moving in with him and Jameson.

* * * *

"Thank God you're okay. I was so upset when I heard about what happened," Freda said as she hugged Mariana and held her tight. Mariana couldn't help the tears that formed in her eyes. She had come to care for Freda so quickly. It was crazy.

"I'm okay," Mariana said and choked up on the tears she was trying to hold back.

Freda smiled, and that was when she noticed the tears in Freda's eyes as well. Mariana couldn't help but wonder if Freda cared about all her escorts this way. She kind of hoped that it was only her that Freda cared this deeply for. Then she cleared her mind. Why was she even thinking such thoughts? She had no right to feel possessive of Freda or her kindness and turn it into something more. Was she suddenly desperate for a family, for someone to love her?

Mariana attempted to step away, but Freda held her hand.

"Let's bring you upstairs to get changed." Mariana glanced at the concerned expressions on Jax's and Jameson's faces. Jax had been acting strangely since he took a private call in his office.

* * * *

Freda waited in the bedroom as Mariana changed back into her regular clothes in the bathroom. She waited patiently, wanting to talk with Mariana about some changes. It seemed that Jax and Jameson did not want her working as an escort any further, but she was committed to a few more dates. Freda could get Mariana out of the commitments, but only if that was what Mariana wanted. It seemed to her that Jax was being extra pushy. Freda knew that both men had intense personalities and were used to giving orders, not taking them, but this was different. They were on edge and they were immediately possessive of Mariana.

The bathroom door opened, and Marian emerged with the dress hanging over her arm.

"I loved this dress. I'm so upset that it was ripped. I'll pay for it somehow. Can you let me know how much it will cost to fix? Maybe Margarete could tell you?"

"Nonsense. It wasn't your fault at all and, believe me, Margarete can fix anything."

Mariana placed it onto the edge of the bed and then she stood there with her hands clasped in front of her.

"There's something I would like to discuss with you. Jax and Jameson informed me that they do not want you being an escort any longer," Freda told her.

Mariana gasped then placed her hands on her hips.

"They can't make a decision like that for me."

"They just did. They're making it quite clear that you belong to them now."

Mariana blushed as she lowered her head. Then she shook it side to side.

"Is this not true? Don't you care for them?"

Mariana looked up.

"I care for them. Too much actually," Mariana said then sat on the edge of the bed. Freda sat on the chair across from the bed, just a few feet in front of her.

"How can you care too much?"

"I don't really even know them. I like them a lot and it's way too soon to have such strong feelings. It frightens me to be honest with you, Freda."

"Of course it does. The power of love between three people is rare."

That statement seemed to make Mariana blush an even darker shade of red. Freda cleared her throat.

"I'm not that old, Mariana. I noticed the change in you immediately upon your arrival. You looked so happy and you were practically glowing with both Jax and Jameson flanking you on either side. They in return looked determined to show their possessiveness and care."

"It's too much. They can't just start telling me what to do and that I can't be an escort. I was counting on that money to help pay my college loans and other stuff."

"You mean the bank loan?"

Mariana's mouth gaped open. "You know about that?"

Freda nodded.

"They know about it, too, and about you having no heat in your apartment. They want to take care of you."

"I have heat in my apartment now. They can't take over my affairs, my burdens. Those are my responsibility and that's why I need to work."

"They care about you greatly. They may be rough around the edges and demanding, but they care and would do anything for you."

"How do you know them so well?"

"Their actions, Mariana. They are good men. Even without you knowing they've already taken on the role of providing for you and bettering your life. You can trust them."

"I think you're mistaken about them providing for me. Yes, they saved me from Ellington's assault and we shared a wonderful night together and I care for them, but I can take care of myself."

"They got the heat turned on in your apartment," Freda told her, and Mariana's eyes widened.

"They did that for me? How?" she asked as her voice cracked.

"They know a lot of people. They were trying to find out about where you worked, so that they could get a delivery from your company and they could talk to you. Alvin told me all about it. He said when he dropped you off that night, the utility trucks were there and the building had heat like never before."

Mariana wiped a tear from her eye.

"They did that for me? We hardly knew one another then," she whispered.

"You have that instant effect on people. Look at me, if I could have a daughter, I'd want her to be like you," Freda admitted as her eyes welled up with tears now, too.

Mariana stared at her a moment then stood up and walked over toward Freda. She knelt down and took Freda's hand into her own.

"You've done so much for me, Freda. None of this would be happening right now if you hadn't offered me the escort job."

"I saw the way that Jax and Jameson looked at you that night at Roldolpho's and I knew that you were meant for them. They've been alone for so long. They've both had hard lives and sad experiences. They closed off their hearts to affection until seeing you."

"I'm scared, Freda. I've had my share of heartache. I lost my mother who really wasn't much of one and I lost the one man I thought loved me. I'm afraid to get hurt. I don't want to think about what could happen if this doesn't work out between me, Jameson, and Jax."

"I think it will work out fine, because it's meant to be. The sooner you realize that you're no longer alone in this world the better."

"But if it doesn't work out, I'll never be the same. No man will ever compare to Jax and Jameson."

"That feeling inside is natural. No one wants to get hurt or to feel loss. But if you hide from the risks in life and in love, then you never get to experience the power of it. Give them a chance. Worse case, if it doesn't work out, you have me," Freda said as a tear rolled down her cheek.

"Oh, Freda," Mariana said then hugged her tightly. "We'll have each other," Mariana whispered, and Freda felt both relief and happiness. Mariana meant more to her than she would ever know.

* * * *

"No, Jax, I am not moving in with you and Jameson." Mariana stomped her foot as she stood in Freda's study along with Jax, Jameson, Freda, and Alvin.

"You are and that is final," Jax stated firmly then stood up as if he had the last word and they were now leaving because he said so.

"No. You have no right to make that decision for me just as you had no right to tell Freda that I am no longer working as an escort. That is my income and I have bills to pay."

"Not anymore," Jameson added as he crossed his arms in front of his chest and stared down at her.

Mariana growled. "What are you talking about? I have college loans to pay and other things. Like rent and bills and—"

"They are all paid for as of thirty minutes ago," Jax said, and Mariana nearly fainted.

"What?" she exclaimed, raising her voice.

"They are. Now, you have a choice, we can stop by your apartment and grab some clothes or the company we hired to do it will grab everything and bring it over to our penthouse. Your choice."

She was so confused. She knew they cared for her, but this was insane. She owed a lot of money. They covered eighty thousand like it was a few hundred bucks. They got her heat turned on in her apartment building because they didn't want her to be cold. They didn't want her working because they wanted to take care of her. Was this a fairy tale come true or a nightmare that would explode in her face with time?

"Say good-bye to Freda and Alvin. We're going home now," Jax whispered.

Mariana looked at Freda who smiled at her, and Alvin looked about to burst into laughter.

"You think this is funny?" she barked, and Alvin and his expression changed and now he looked stern, too.

"Do as your men say. They care for you and getting out of that neighborhood sounds great to me." With that, Alvin walked out of the room.

Mariana was in shock. Even Alvin didn't like her neighborhood and seemed angry that she lived there.

"You call me later about the jobs next weekend."

"She's done, Freda," Jameson interrupted.

"I will let you know. Thank you for everything." Mariana hugged Freda good-bye then followed Jax from her home. She was trying to think of what to say to Jax and Jameson as they got into their Range Rover.

As they headed out for the nice area of Houston, she knew they were headed toward her apartment building.

"I don't want you to see it," she whispered from the backseat.

Jameson turned around to look at her. Jax glanced to her from the rearview mirror. His dark-blue eyes looked intense as usual.

"There's nothing to be ashamed of. You've had to sacrifice a lot. You've been on your own and, as you said, alone to fend for yourself. You're done being alone. You're done starving from not having enough money or the ability to take care of your health. We're taking over. We're taking care of you and it's because we care. Get used to it."

Great, now Jameson was acting just like Jax. She didn't dare reply what was going through her head. She didn't want to be bossed around, yet knowing that they paid off her loans, her mother's bills, and turned on her heat made her feel aroused. She was losing her ever-loving mind.

They did this to her. They made her feel appreciated, sexy, and alive from their possessive behavior. If she were smart, she would exert some form of independence and not allow them to think that they could tell her what to do with every aspect of her life. The more she thought that they wanted her to be their puppet the angrier she became. By the time they pulled up to her apartment building and parked the car then entered the crappy entryway, she felt the fight within her diminish.

One look over her shoulder at Jax and Jameson and she could sense their disappointment and disgust with the place. As they climbed the three flights of stairs since the elevator was out of service as usual, she noticed that her apartment door was unlocked.

"Oh no," she exclaimed, and immediately Jameson was placing her behind him and both men pulled out guns.

"Where did you get those? What are you doing?" she asked in a panic. They were carrying guns all morning and she had no idea?

Jax entered, and she feared that he could get hurt, but then again, they were professional. She was probably robbed because she didn't come home last night. Someone was watching her place waiting for the opportunity to break in.

Jax walked back a few seconds later.

His search was fast, but her apartment was so freaking small the tour was as quick as a hiccup.

"It's all clear, but the place is a mess. Completely ransacked."

"Oh God."

Jameson pulled her into his arms and hugged her.

"There's not much to salvage, honey. Clothes are torn up. I think we should call the police and bring you back down to the Rover," Jax said then stared at Jameson. She noticed the exchange of looks, and it bothered her. Something told her that he wasn't telling her everything.

"Wait, I want to see."

Jameson pulled her back, kind of hard.

"Let the police come. They might be able to fingerprint the place and find out who was responsible."

"No. I want to look."

She pulled from Jameson and pushed open the door. The place was a complete mess and appeared as if a bomb exploded in it. The further she walked in the more it became clear that nothing was taken, it was just destroyed.

She walked to her bedroom and gasped, covering her mouth.

The words "DIE BITCH" were painted in red on the walls and the letters dripped like blood. A brown knife was sticking into the pillow. Her bras and panties were ripped to shreds.

Jameson wrapped an arm around her waist and pulled her out of the room. She could hear Jax talking into the phone.

"Get them here now. Jameson is taking Mariana back to our place."

Chapter 11

Mariana sat on the couch with her feet tucked under her butt and a blanket over her. She was waiting on hold on the phone for someone at the college's main office to assist her with replacing her textbooks. She had just paid for the ones she was using.

She couldn't get the images out of her head. The bloody words, the torn garments. Everything she owned was destroyed. All her clothing, her crappy furniture, her books for school. Everything. Who would do something like this?

"Who are you on the phone with?" Jameson asked as he stormed into the room. He looked fierce as he grabbed the phone from her hands and disconnected the call. She jumped up, the blanket fell from her shoulders, and she yelled at him.

"Why did you do that? I've been on hold for fifteen damn minutes with the college main office."

"For what?" he asked, not even caring that she yelled at him and was angry. He was acting pompous.

"I need new books and a new schedule and study guide. I have an exam on Thursday that I need to study for and that was destroyed by whomever ransacked my apartment. You had no right doing that."

He closed the space between them in no time at all. He pulled her into his arms, she gasped for breath, and he squeezed her to him.

"Fuck!" He growled as he lifted her up so that she was forced to straddle his waist.

She knew something was terribly wrong. They were all on edge, obviously, but Jameson had disappeared for a while, saying he had phone calls to make and Jax still hadn't returned from her apartment. She was worried, and they were both uptight.

Mariana pulled back and cupped Jameson's face between her hands. "What is it? What's going on?"

She could practically see the struggle going on in his eyes and facial expression. He was worried.

"Baby, I just can't get the images out of my head. The words on the wall, the knife in the damn pillow. What if you left last night and went back there without us?"

She hadn't even thought about that. She was still trying to recover from Ellington's assault.

"I didn't even think about that, Jameson. Don't make yourself crazy worrying about the things that could have happened. I was here with you and Jax. I was safe."

He squeezed her tighter, and she felt his hand cup under her ass. She was so small compared to him. She felt feminine and delicate in his embrace.

"You're staying here with us. This is your home now," he said through clenched teeth. This wasn't the type of invite she would hope for if she was going to take a chance on this type of relationship. She took an unsteady breath.

"I don't have anywhere else to go. I was barely paying the rent there."

"Remember, we took care of your bills. There aren't any more. Look at this as a fresh start. Jax and I want to take care of you. We want you here with us."

She thought about his words and how it felt to be in his arms.

"I don't really know you at all."

He moved toward the couch and sat down, with her still in his arms and straddling his waist.

"What do you want to know?"

"Do you have a family, or parents?"

"No. But we do have some close friends of ours we were in the Marines with. They live outside of the city. They actually own a really cool restaurant and bar with their fathers."

"What's it called?"

"Casper's. It's really nice and they have a bunch of pictures from boot camp and other places they were stationed. Their dads were in the military as well."

"Dads? You mean like more than one? How can that be?"

He ran the palms of his hands up and down her thighs. Despite the jean material she felt the warmth penetrate right through to her skin.

"Baby, they're a family. John Luke, Jasper, and Davie married Eve and they had three sons, our buddies, Garrett, Gunner, and Wes. Maybe we'll take a trip out there this weekend. We have a house about twenty minutes from Casper's. It's on a nice parcel of land. It's really beautiful and peaceful there."

"You own this penthouse and a house with land?" she asked.

He smiled at her. "We've worked really hard for our money, baby. I invented that panic button plus a bunch of other things that help soldiers in combat and spies," he teased as he squeezed her hips then pulled her close and kissed her. At least she thought he was teasing.

"How long were you in the military?"

He got awfully quiet as he caressed her hair away from her face and kept his hand on her shoulder and against her neck. Once again, his hold was possessive. It seemed both brothers liked to hold her in ways that made her feel cherished yet also sexy.

"I was in for a little under fourteen years."

"Fourteen years? How old were you when you enlisted? How old are you now?"

"I enlisted when I was twenty. Jax was almost twenty-three at the time and already enlisted. We were living on our own, trying to survive. We were doing okay but we wanted more. We wanted college education and careers. We figured we could join the service and get our education but it turned into so much more. We both have our masters degrees. Mine is in biotechnology and Jax's is in engineering. But we loved serving in the military as commandoes. We have special abilities and we used those to run and maintain our security company."

"I'm really impressed and you invented that panic button, too. That is amazing. I don't even have my bachelors degree yet. I've been taking classes when I can, but I'm already twenty-four."

"You're young enough and determined to get that degree. You'll do it. You're going for a business degree, right?"

"Yes. I want to run my own art gallery one day. But I think now, I'll settle for just being a director of one. But there aren't any jobs in that. At least at none of the galleries around here."

Jameson smiled.

"Maybe something will pop up sooner than later."

She shrugged her shoulders.

"What about you? Any family or old boyfriends that might show up looking to reclaim what's ours?" he asked as he squeezed her hips then ran the palms of his hands up her chest to cup her breasts. She absorbed the feel of his large hands, and then his fingers pinched the material of her bra, trying to pinch her nipples.

She lowered her head and closed her eyes. She couldn't help but feel sad. She had asked Jameson to tell her about his life and Jax's, and now she should share more about her own.

"My dad left my mom when I was three. Not sure why, but she always said he cheated on her and that he was a drunk. But my mom wasn't any better if that was the case. By the time I was fifteen, she was doing drugs. Prescription drugs actually. I was working by then, waiting on tables and babysitting and trying to go to school. High school sucked because we didn't have a lot of money and I didn't have a lot of clothes. Anyway, by the time I started applying for college, her habit got worse and she started bringing home money, telling me that when I was in school she was working."

Jameson rubbed her thighs again and held her gaze.

"I actually thought she was involved in prostitution. She never brought anyone home but she would get dressed in this very tight, sexy dress and leave. Sometimes for days at a time."

"What did you do about food?"

"I lived on raw hot dogs and whatever I could bring home from the diner I worked at. The boss was a jerk. He didn't allow anything to be taken for free and I didn't want to spend my money. Anyway, in a matter of a few months, my mom got arrested for possession and selling. She was locked up for a while. I would visit her in jail, but then I graduated high school and wanted to go to college. I stuck around here because of her. I guess I hoped that she would get better. You know, maybe wake up and see that doing drugs was wrong and that I needed a mother. No such luck."

"What happened to her?"

Mariana thought about it. How her mom looked and how she found a dirty needle lying on the tile floor and an empty prescription bottle next to her mom.

Mariana tried to get up off of Jameson's lap, but he didn't allow it. He gave her hips a little jerk and a squeeze.

"I want to know."

"I'll never forget that day. I came in from working all night. One of the other girls didn't show and my boss made me work her shift. I needed money for books for college so I stayed. If I hadn't, who knows if my mom would have shot up and took the pills."

"What?"

"I found her on the tile floor."

"Oh, baby. Shit, I'm sorry."

"She was so gray and old looking. Her hair was greasy. There was a rubber strap around her upper arm and a dirty needle on the floor next to her. There was also an empty prescription bottle. She died from either an overdose or just too many different drugs in her system."

"I'm so sorry you had to see that, Mariana. I couldn't even imagine having to witness something like that."

"It doesn't matter now. She's gone and she wasn't much of a mother anyhow. She left me that damn loan she took out. It was a constant reminder of her habit, her life, and all she hadn't given to me as a mother."

"That's gone now, Mariana. No more bills laying over your head."

She held his gaze and placed her hands on his shoulders.

"I wish you hadn't done that. It was so much money and it wasn't your burden, it was mine."

"You don't seem to get it, do you? We care about you. A lot. We take care of those we care about and you needed the help. We don't want you working so much while you're trying to get your degree. We want you to have time and energy to be with Jax and I," he said then winked and smiled.

She couldn't help but to blush then smile back.

"Are you two for real?"

He squinted his one eye at her.

"What is that supposed to mean?"

"I'm a bit of a pessimist, I guess. Experience has shown me that sometimes things aren't always as they appear and people can change right before your very eyes."

"You don't trust me or Jax?"

"It's not trust per se. It's more like fear of history repeating itself."

"Go on and explain."

"There's nothing to explain."

"Who was he and how did he hurt you?"

She was shocked. How the heck did he figure a man was involved? She shrugged her shoulders and told him about Gavan.

"What an asshole. But, it worked out. You belong with us, not him."

She hesitated to be completely honest with him. Even doing that scared her. Opening up her heart for pain and admitting her fears would give him and Jax power over her. Her heart battled her mind. She had taught herself to not rely on anyone. Too many people promised faith, commitment then failed to come through. Would Jax and Jameson be different? Could she trust them?

She felt his fingers under her chin as he tilted her face toward his. She locked gazes with his dark-blue eyes. "Hey, you got awfully quiet. What's wrong?"

"Honestly?"

He smiled softly. Her heart melted, and that feeling of distrust slowly diminished.

"Honesty is important in a relationship."

There he was talking about relationships again. Could they really want her?

"Are you sure you want to be in a relationship with me?"

His thumb caressed across her lower lip.

"As sure as I've ever been about anything in my life. It's simple. It's right."

"How do you know?"

He squinted his eyes at her a moment.

"Baby, you really have a difficult time trusting people, don't you?"

She didn't reply. She didn't need to as she held her serious expression.

"What are you so afraid of with Jax and I?"

Her heart raced. She felt her hands become clammy as she swallowed hard. *Honesty. I have to tell the truth and if they hurt me in the end, then I will once again be alone in a world waiting to eat me whole.*

"I can't help but be fearful that you'll leave me, too. For something or someone better."

He placed his palm against her cheek and held her gaze. "Baby, we won't leave you or hurt you, because you are meant for us. Jax and I have never felt like this about anyone, ever. I know trust is difficult for you, and after what you shared with me I can understand why. But, you need to trust me. I won't leave you and neither will Jax."

She hugged him tight and felt the tears well up in her eyes.

"I couldn't stand it if you left me. Either of you," she admitted, and he squeezed her to him then began to kiss her cheek. She pulled back, and he covered her mouth with his own.

She immediately felt Jameson's hands move up and under her shirt. He released her lips a moment to pull her shirt over her head. The feel of his strong, large hands pressing against her skin, maneuvering her to his liking, aroused her senses. He explored her mouth with his tongue while nimble fingers unclasped her bra. Pulling his lips from hers he continued to kiss her, spreading loving along her jaw and neck as he lifted her by the hips so he could feast on her bare breast.

"Oh, Jameson," she whispered, running her fingers through his hair, pressing her breast firmer against his mouth. He nipped and pulled on her nipple, making her panties wet as desperation filled her.

She clawed at his shirt. Pulled the fabric upward causing him to abandon her needy breast with a pop.

"I want you now. Right here." His words, his tone were typical Jameson commanding. In a flash they were divesting one another of their clothing.

She stood in awe, breathing rapidly as she took in the sight of her man. Jameson was filled with muscles from his firm jaw to his thick, long cock.

He lay down on the ottoman, his legs hung over the sides, spread wide. Even his thighs had muscles and were sexy. She climbed right up on top of him as he fisted his cock and lined it up with her pussy.

"Now," he demanded, and she complied. She adjusted her body over his cock and took him in slowly. It was exquisite torture but obviously too much for Jameson. His fingers dug into her hips and he shoved her downward as he thrust upward. Their bodies clashed and united together.

Mariana screamed. Jameson tightened up and held her there as he took unsteady breaths. He spoke through clenched teeth.

"You feel so tight and perfect, baby. Inside you I'm home."

Up and down, she began to ride him, trying to find her release as if desperate for all of Jameson. They moaned and petted one another. He cupped her breasts. She tweaked his nipples as she thrust her hips, feeling him grow larger and larger inside of her.

The sound of footsteps grabbed their attention. She tensed a moment until Jameson jerked her hips.

"On me. You focus on me and nothing else."

His demand was intense, and she wondered if this was a time, a test to trust him.

Jameson pulled on her nipple hard. So hard she felt the pinch of pain and screamed right before the gush of fluid lubricated his cock.

"That's it. You like it a little rough don't you?" he asked her as he pulled hard on her other nipple eliciting another cry from her. She sensed movement to the side of her, but before Mariana could turn to see who was there, Jameson grabbed her by her hair, pulling her down for a deep and wild kiss. His tongue stroked the cavern of her mouth. She tried to keep up as their tongues battled for control, and then she felt the hand on her ass and the cool liquid against her puckered hole. She jerked, but Jameson wouldn't let her up.

"I need you, Mariana. Now. Like this," Jax whispered as he cupped her thighs, squeezing, arousing her anus and preparing her for double penetration.

She moaned against Jameson's mouth, and then she felt the thick, bulbous head of Jax's cock against her back opening.

The palms of his hands caressed up her spine and then back down as he parted her ass cheeks and pushed through. Jameson held her thighs and ass, adding to the excitement of both men touching her and making love to her together.

"I need this. I need you," Jax said then began to move in and out of her ass. Jameson released her lips as she panted with her face flat against his shoulder.

"Oh God, Jax, it's too much."

"No. Never too much. You're mine. Ours," he said so strongly she shook, and he moved faster. He grabbed onto her hips and thrust into her so damn deep she screamed. Her body exploded immediately, and then both men began to move together. Up and down, in and out, they took complete control of her body and branded her their woman.

Both men roared as they thrust together inside of her and exploded. She felt their bodies shake, and their breathing sounded as raspy as her own, but she closed her eyes and relished in the aftermath. She was their woman and they were her men. She hoped that this was forever.

* * * *

Jax slowly pulled from Mariana's body and walked away. Jameson caressed her hair and continued to kiss her skin until Jax returned. Jameson knew that something was up. Jax was kind of rough, the way he took Mariana's ass. She was new to anal sex, and he wanted to make certain that they didn't hurt her. She was precious and needed reassurance that they were her protectors and lovers and not the enemy.

"Are you okay?" he asked her, and she moaned but remained lying over his chest. Her long, wavy brown hair was damp from perspiration.

He caressed over her lower back and ass. He trailed a finger along the crevice. "Are you sure?" he asked. She nodded slightly as he looked over her shoulder at a very angry Jax.

"I didn't hurt her." He barked.

"I was just making sure. She's new to this."

"I know that. Don't you think I know that? I would never hurt her."

"You need to calm down."

Jax released an annoyed sigh, and Mariana slowly lifted her head up.

"What's wrong?" she asked Jax, and he ran his fingers through his hair as he stood there in a pair of navy-blue boxers.

He took a deep breath then slowly released it.

"Nothing. I'm sorry." He walked closer and caressed her back and then her ass as he knelt down beside the ottoman.

"I missed you." He cupped her face between his hands and kissed her.

When he released her lips, she lay back down with her cheek against Jameson's chest. Jameson locked gazes with Jax and immediately he knew that something triggered Jax's behavior and his need to possess Mariana.

"Hey, baby, why don't you let Jax start a hot bath for you? You can soak a bit while we shower up."

"Mmm, sounds good."

Jameson looked at Jax, and Jax nodded his head as he caressed Mariana's back and ass before standing up and heading to the bathroom. While she was in there, Jameson and Jax could talk about what exactly was going on.

* * * *

"Okay, so spit it out," Jameson said as he towel dried his hair. Jax had already showered and now sat on the couch in the living room.

"We've got ourselves a bit of a situation."

"With Mariana's apartment being ransacked?"

"It was a message. Spider thinks that it was meant for us."

Jameson sat on the couch with the towel in his hands. They were both dressed in dress pants and shirts.

"What does that mean?"

"He thinks that this has something to do with our business dealings. Someone may be trying to scare us into not becoming so large so quickly. Not sure really."

"Maybe he's wrong," Jameson suggested.

Jax shook his head as he looked at the rug and then back up toward his brother.

"The knife was custom made. Under the pillow was a typed note. It said, 'We can get to her any time we want to.'"

"Fuck!" Jameson stated then stood up.

"Exactly. Someone wants to scare us."

"Well, they just fucking did scare us. What are we going to do?"

"Our jobs, for one, and take care of Mariana. We can't let her out of our sights."

"She has school."

"Fuck school. She doesn't need to go."

"She does, Jax. She's been working so hard for her degree. It means so much to her. Plus there's more. We talked while you were gone."

"Talked about what?"

"Us, and our intentions," Jameson said, and then he told Jax all about Marian's upbringing and her fears.

"She needs us, Jameson."

"Exactly and we need her, too. I don't care what all this shit is about. If it means we have to close up shop, I'll do it. We've got more than enough money to live life multiple times in luxury. She's more important than anything. And, not sure if you realized it or not, but we haven't been using any protection with her."

Jax ran his fingers through his hair. "I know. I thought about it for a split second and then it hit me. I want her forever. I don't want to lose her. I want her pregnant with our children."

"I don't want to scare her, Jax. She's younger than us. She has goals and expectations."

"She loves us already. She's just scared like we are. The power of our connection is incredible, Jameson. I want this. But right now our priority is her protection We need to keep her out of harm's way."

"We need to take her out of the city then."

"I agree. I also have this feeling that we're missing something with this. It's got to be more than coincidental that Clover Masters was trying to steal your ideas."

"You think Clover is behind this incident at Mariana's?"

"I'm not sure, but Spider and the guys are investigating. He thinks we should take Mariana out of town for a couple of weeks."

"How is she supposed to attend school?"

"She can't."

"That's not fair to her, Jax. If Clover or whomever wants to go after us through Mariana, then we need to protect her. But taking her away from her studies, just isn't fair for her."

"I don't care. She's our woman and our responsibility. You said it yourself. We need her as much as she needs us. Besides, we know the dean of that college. He attends some of the art galleries at Roldolpho's. I'm sure if we explain the situation that he would get her professors to send along the work so she can do it online. She only has a semester to go," Jax stated with confidence.

"Fine. Whatever you think is best. But what about Clover?"

"I have men on him now. If he's up to something, then we'll know it soon enough."

* * * *

"I can't allow you to buy me a whole new wardrobe," Mariana said as she stood in the laundry room and waited for her jeans to dry. She had one outfit to her name. The T-shirt and jeans she changed into at Freda's place.

"You are so damn stubborn." Jax raised his voice at her, and she glared at him. She wasn't backing down.

"Here. This is from Freda," Jameson interrupted, stretching his arm between Jax and Mariana to pass along an envelope. She took it and stared at him.

"What is it?"

"Your pay from the other night."

Mariana looked inside the envelope and gasped. There were five thousand dollars in it.

Jax and Jameson looked just as shocked and a bit angry to boot.

"What exactly did you and Theo do on that date?" Jax asked.

She held his gaze. "Nothing."

"Nothing?" Jameson now questioned her.

"Hey, it's not that type of escort service. Besides, I was actually kind of on my own most of the time. Theo is quite popular."

"Which is how Ellington got you alone. Let's not think about it," Jax said then walked out of the room.

"Freda did say that Theo gave you a little extra. I think maybe he felt bad about leaving you alone and giving Ellington the opportunity to strike."

"I can't accept this. It's five thousand dollars."

Mariana was in shock.

"That's a drop in the bucket to Theo. Believe me," Jameson added then walked out of the room.

Just then the dryer buzzed. Her only pair of pants were dry. Why were Jameson and Jax so upset about the money? She did do her job. She stared at the envelope then place it down as she dropped the towel from around her, reached into the dryer, and took out her clothing. As she was buttoning her jeans she sensed someone standing by the doorway watching her. It was Jameson.

"You're finished being an escort. You know that, right? We're not allowing it. That part of your life is over."

Her first reaction was to snap at him. How dare he tell her what she can and can't do. But then she knew that they worried about her and cared. She didn't want to risk getting caught in a situation again that she couldn't handle.

She nodded her head as she put her shirt on.

"We're taking a little trip. We'll grab some clothes on the way and more once we get to our house."

She stared at him. "We're going to your house in the suburbs? The one with all the land?"

He nodded his head.

"Wait. For how long? I have a test on Friday."

"That's taken care of. You can work off of my laptop."

"Wait a minute. What do you mean 'taken care of'? What did you do?" she asked, feeling the anger fill her immediately.

Jameson stared at her in such a way that it made her belly do a series of somersaults and her gut clench. He was acting differently. Something wasn't right.

"Jax spoke with the dean. Your professors have been notified. We set up an e-mail account for your assignments to be sent and any work needed." Her jaw dropped.

"The dean? You know the dean?" She didn't know if she should scream or just hit something. How dare they take control of her life like this. "You can't be serious. You didn't interfere in my life like that? You're joking around."

He glanced at his watch, dismissing her attitude and anger as if he were bored with her upset.

"Get ready. We leave in fifteen minutes."

"Wait." She grabbed his arm. He stared down into her eyes.

"Why did Jax do that? Why are you taking over my life?" she asked as her voice cracked.

He swallowed hard then placed his hands on her shoulders.

"Remember when we talked about trust?"

She nodded her head.

"You need to trust Jax and I right now. We're doing what is best for you. We're trying to keep you safe." He kissed her forehead then escorted her from the laundry room. Mariana couldn't help but wonder what, or whom, it was that they were keeping her safe from.

Chapter 12

"It seems like your plan worked, Clover. The Spauldings left town an hour ago. My sources say they notified their office that they would be gone a week or two."

Clover smiled at Buster's news.

"That is perfect. Now, there's no way they can connect the apartment thing to me, right?"

"No way, sir. I had some shits from that neighborhood take care of things. It cost a few hundred but it was worth it. It seems like the Spaulding brothers really care about Mariana. So much for virginal and sweet and innocent, huh? Fucking two guys like that."

"I have to admit that I hadn't seen that coming."

"Well it's not too uncommon, but still, she's hot. It makes her more appealing, I think, knowing that she can handle two guys their size at once."

Clover squinted his eyes and clasped his hands under his chin. She could be a bonus to really seek some revenge on Jameson and Jax. Maybe he could steal her away from them, rip off Darian Rothesburgh, skip town, and take the girl, too? She was probably fantastic in bed and maybe she would like it as rough as he enjoyed it. No other women had been able to keep up with his bedroom fantasies.

"I don't like that look, boss."

"I'm thinking of adding some things to the plan."

"Things, sir?"

"Yes, Buster. I want you to try and keep an eye on where they take Mariana. I want to know when she returns, which I am assuming will be for the gala in two weeks. Jameson and Jax especially are really into art. Even though they didn't get the security detail, they'll attend."

"And why do you want her followed?"

"I'm thinking that she may be a great going-away gift for me. You know, someone who can possibly handle being in my bed."

Buster's eyes widened. "No other woman had been able to thus far."

"She's special. As you said, handling two men as big as those two at once is interesting and appealing, don't you think?"

Buster smirked. "I'll take care of it, boss. When do you want to nab her?"

"As soon as the artwork is securely in the trucks and safely out of town. She'll be there, too. So maybe that will be the time to take her. While you're at it, get rid of the snitch in X-Caliber's organization. We don't need her anymore either. Make it so that no one ever finds her."

"Very good, sir. I'll start planning accordingly."

Clover smiled as he thought about the new life that lay ahead of him and the new brunette that would be in his bed soon enough.

* * * *

Mariana was tired of arguing with Jax and Jameson over shopping for clothes. She picked out the necessities and then tried to pay for them with her own money and they flipped out. They totally made a scene in the store and she was embarrassed into letting them pay for stuff. With a trunk full of new clothing and shoes, she finally convinced them that they could head out of town and to what they referred to as their small getaway retreat house.

After leaving the city and seeing all the small houses, it reminded her of home. Not that her mom and her place was special. It was old, crappy, had a roof that leaked, and a damp mildew-like smell in the spring, but it was still her home. It was the only one she ever had.

Mariana closed her eyes and thought about her mother. She hadn't been back to her graveside since the day, before the night of her first escort job. She wasn't even sure why she went there. Maybe because she didn't have anyone else to talk to, or to tell about the new job? Maybe because she hoped that her life would change for the better and she would have a chance to make some money, save some money, and get her dream job.

"Hey, baby, you're awfully quiet. Tired from shopping?" Jameson asked as he turned sideways in the seat.

"Just thinking."

"About what?" Jax asked, in a rather sharp tone. She was coming to realize that Jax was hard and abrupt more often than not. She still wondered about this trip and its real purpose.

"Actually, thinking about when I was a kid. Growing up in a neighborhood like the ones we passed a while back. As rundown as it was, I still called it home. Haven't felt like home anywhere else since. I guess someday I will."

"We want you to think of us as home, baby. Wherever we are."

She smiled at that comment from Jameson. He was sweet.

A while later they pulled up to a gated community, with huge houses that were acres apart. They traveled along the roads passing house after house, small mansion after small mansion, and then to another gate with a large *S* decorating the center. Another long driveway and there it stood. Their very large, very country-looking estate. It was modern, yet rustic with stone and wood siding. The double burgundy doors were gorgeous, and in the center was that signature *S*, again. *Spaulding. The* S *is for their name. This is their country home.*

Jax parked the car, and Jameson opened the door for her to get out. She was in awe of the beauty both of the home and the surrounding open land. There was a gorgeous wraparound porch that was extra wide, and she could just imagine sitting out there in the warmer months, reading a book or enjoying the property.

"This is gorgeous," she said, and Jameson smiled.

"I'm glad that you like it."

"Like it? What's not to like, Jameson? It is stunning and I love that porch."

"Come on, let's head inside. It's kind of cold out here," Jax said, and they climbed the four steps of the porch as Jax unlocked then opened the front door. He disarmed the alarm system, and they headed inside. There was so much to see. The floor-to-ceiling stone fireplace, the large entertainment center and flat-screen television, and the open floor plan. She twirled around noticing the high ceilings and the winding staircase that led upstairs to a second floor.

"This place is huge," she blurted out then walked into the living room and ran her hand across the soft fabric of the earth-tone sectional.

"Ruth left the refrigerator well stocked and dinner is in the oven staying warm," Jax said as he folded up a piece of paper after coming from another hallway.

"Great. I thought I smelled her famous roasted chicken," Jameson added, and Mariana wondered who Ruth was. She felt that tinge of jealousy in her gut. Her facial expression must have been obvious to them. Both men were immediately next to her.

"Are you okay? What is it?" Jax asked.

"Nothing," she replied then tried to move along and explore the house. Jax grabbed her hand and pulled her back toward him.

"Something upset you. What was it?"

She lowered her eyes to the floor. Jax touched her chin and tilted it up toward him.

"It's none of my business."

"Honesty, Mariana, remember?" Jameson added with his hands on his hips and a serious expression on his face. These two men had such an effect on her. It was scary.

"It's none of my business who Ruth is. It's no big deal. We're not even really seeing one another. I understand." She tried to turn away, and Jax yanked her back and against his chest. He held her hands behind her back with one of his much larger hands.

With his free hand he held her jaw and cheek. He stared down into her eyes.

"Ruth is the housekeeper. You belong to Jameson and I just as we belong to you. There's no other woman and there sure as hell better not ever be another man. Got it?"

She swallowed hard, and he squeezed her wrists then kissed her deeply on the mouth. Very quickly that kiss turned into more, and in no time at all, they were naked and she was bent over the soft couch she admired when they first arrived.

She felt Jax lean over her. His body was pressed snug against her own as he thrust his cock under her slit. He moved back and forth, torturing her. Did he want her to beg for it?

She felt his warm breath against her neck and ear. She gripped the couch tighter. She felt so overtaken with lust.

"I'm not a mushy, sit-down-and-talk-for-hours kind of guy," he said then ran his fingers through her hair. He gripped a handful, making her look into his eyes and hold his gaze as his lips touched her lower lip. "I'm only going to tell you this once. There're no other women. I'm falling in love with you and there'll never be anyone else but you, Mariana. Ever."

He licked her lip then sucked it between his lips and devoured her moans. Simultaneously, he entered her from behind in one quick stroke. His words, his actions took her breath away.

Jameson joined them. He knelt on the couch underneath where her chest and head hung forward, and he turned her toward him by placing his hands against her cheeks. He smiled.

"You belong to us. This is real. So stop holding back and accept your feelings for us."

He lifted up, his cock inches from her lips, and she knew exactly what he wanted.

Relaxing her throat as Jax continued to pump into her from behind as he massaged her shoulders, she opened wide and began to take Jameson's cock into her mouth for the very first time.

She felt so sexual and a bit naughty. Especially as she worked her tongue and lips around Jameson's cock and he moaned in pleasure.

"Fuck, baby, that mouth is incredible."

She moved up and down in synch to Jax's thrusts. Jax was grunting behind her, and Jameson was holding her hair, trying to control her movements.

"Slow down, baby, or I'm going to lose it," Jameson said through clenched teeth.

It was too late. She was losing control herself. She felt hungry, wild with need as she bobbed her head up and down and then Jax shoved forward and exploded inside of her. She gasped, and Jameson pulled from her mouth. In a flash Jax was pulling out of her and Jameson was grabbing her over the couch. She squealed and somehow wound up on her back on top of the ottoman as Jameson moved between her legs.

"I love you, Mariana," he said through clenched teeth then thrust into her. She reached for him, held on to his shoulders as he pounded into her pussy, stroking her inner muscles, making her explode once again. She could hardly catch her breath. She felt overwhelmed and emotional when Jameson climaxed. Three more fast pumps into her then he collapsed against her, squeezing her hard.

When they finally calmed their breathing, Jameson slowly pulled from her body and played with her breasts. He smiled down at her.

"You're incredible. I'm never going to let you go."

* * * *

It was after they made love and after the heat of passion that she lay in Jax's arms and imagined living here with him and Jameson and starting a family. As she thought about children and working, she thought about the many times they made love without protection. Her heart raced, and she wondered if Jax and Jameson knew exactly what they were doing or if all three of them were so overtaken with lust that it never crossed their minds. Now she would have something more to worry about. The fear of being a single mom now ruled over her happy thoughts. But then came their words of love and of commitment. She was confused. They were going to go out tonight to meet friends of Jameson and Jax's. Perhaps when they got home, she could bring up her concerns. She wanted them. She wanted to feel like this, loved, satisfied, safe, forever.

* * * *

"You are so full of shit, Jax. I was fucking there. I remember dragging your ass out of that building in the nick of time." Gunner raised his voice, and the men roared with laughter. Mariana didn't know who to believe with all the crazy war stories they were telling. Gunner, Garrett, and Wes McCallister were ragging on Jax and Jamison for the past hour, and Jax and Jameson were doing the same thing to the McCallisters.

"They'll go on forever about this. My men are stubborn," Gia, their girlfriend, said as she stood by the wall next to Mariana. Gia was really nice. She was tough, but sweet, and Mariana couldn't help but notice how her men adored her. Casper's was a really nice bar and restaurant. Jax and Jameson were right, the McCallister brothers and fathers really did decorate the walls with actual photos of soldiers.

"Hey, did you see the pictures of Jax and Jameson in uniform? There are a few over here. Come on," Gia said as she took Mariana's hand and led her to another wall down past the crowded bar. A glance over her shoulder and she immediately noticed both Jax's and Jameson's eyes on her and the McCallister men's eyes on their woman. Mariana swallowed hard. She was only walking to the other side of the room, so why did she feel so lost without them next to her?

"See, check these out," Gia said and pointed to a series of photos.

Mariana smiled as she looked at two very handsome and very young-looking faces.

"Jameson and Jax look like teenagers."

"They pretty much were. Same with my men. They entered the military young."

Mariana smiled. Gia was really nice. She never had a close friend before. There was never anyone around long enough to trust, but for some odd reason, she felt comfortable with Gia.

"Hey, do you like martial arts?" Gia asked.

"Me?" Mariana asked, wide-eyed. Gia chuckled.

"The reason I ask is that I work out at a place near the gym the guys belong to. It's a great dojo. Maybe tomorrow afternoon you'd like to go to one of the classes I help out in?" Gia asked.

"Really? I've never done anything like that before. I don't even work out."

Gia looked at her sideways.

"Honey, with your body, you have to engage in some serious aerobic activity. You look like an athlete."

Mariana smiled.

"I skateboard."

"Shit, seriously? My God wait until Dale finds out. He'll have you hanging out with his high school buddies, jumping railings and working the skate park down the road."

Mariana laughed.

"How did you get into skateboarding?" Gia asked as they walked over to another spot near the bar and two empty seats.

"It was my only means of transportation. I skateboarded to school, and even in college, and up until a few weeks ago, I was a courier in the city, so skateboarding got me around."

"That is so cool. Do you know how to drive a car?"

"I have a driver's license. I took driver's ed in high school because it was required, but other than driving my ex-boyfriend's car around Houston a bit, I really don't have much experience driving."

"Do you think your men will let me steal you for a couple of hours tomorrow for the dojo?"

Mariana looked over her shoulder at the table where Jax and Jameson sat. Both men were watching her. She smiled, and Jameson gave a small smile, not Jax. He was always so serious. She turned back to Gia.

"Maybe they will. We'll ask them."

* * * *

"So, that's one special young woman you two old men snagged," Wes teased Jax and Jameson.

"Old men?" Jameson asked.

"You're robbing the cradle with that one," Gunner added then took a slug of beer.

"Fuck you. We could say the same for you three and Gia. What is she, like twenty-one?"

"Twenty-four," Garrett replied as he glanced toward where Gia and Mariana sat talking to one another.

Jax was relieved that she felt comfortable here. She was quiet and untrusting.

"Gia and Mariana are the same age," Jameson said.

"Exactly and Jax is what, like forty?" Gunner teased.

"Go to hell. I can still whip your ass," Jax said very seriously. He knew his friends were teasing, and truth was, Jax felt really relaxed being here. Casper's had an atmosphere that reminded him of good times, close friends, and family.

"I can still shoot better than you," Gunner replied.

"Don't let your name go to your head. You're not the best shot around here. I am and always will be," Jax stated.

"Think again, bro. I've got you all beat," Jameson added this time, and they all laughed.

"Sounds like a challenge to me," Wes said.

"You're on, Jameson and Jax. We can hit the shooting range tomorrow and see," Gunner stated.

"All bets are on," Wes said, and they starting carrying on until Jax noticed Mariana and Gia coming toward the table. Gia walked over toward her men, and Garrett grabbed her around the waist and pulled her onto his lap. Jameson did the same to Mariana as he lifted her up and wrapped his arms around her tight. Jax couldn't help but smile at her as he placed his hand on her knee.

"If it's okay with you and Jameson, Jax, I'd like to pick Mariana up tomorrow around ten and bring her to the dojo. I'm helping to run a training class there. Then we can grab a light lunch."

"That sounds like a great idea. While you two young ladies are at the dojo, we're going to the shooting range to solve a little misunderstanding," Garrett said as he emphasized the word "young." Jax and Jameson shook their heads and chuckled.

"What misunderstanding?" Gia asked.

"Don't worry, baby, I have to put these men in their place and prove to them that I'm still the best shot out of all of them," Gunner said as he leaned back in his chair, appearing confident and cocky.

"Not going to happen. You'll see," Jameson added then kissed Mariana's shoulder. Jax smiled to himself. He could get used to this. Relaxing with old friends, seeing Mariana look content with hopefully a new friend, and living out in the country and away from the chaos and aggravation. With thoughts of the city came concerns over the company and over Mariana's safety. Perhaps learning a few self-defense moves or some martial arts wasn't such a bad idea for Mariana after all. His chest tightened at the thought. He and his brother were her protectors now. No one would ever hurt her again.

Chapter 13

I'm not sure about this," Mariana said as she attempted to get out from under Shane, a friend of Gia's and Sensei Lee's. She was definitely in a precarious position as they all attempted to teach Mariana self-defense moves.

"Just keep the pressure on his ribs. Tire him out. Then when you have the opportunity, you strike," Sensei stated.

"Gunny, don't!" Mariana heard Gia yell and as she glanced behind her, she saw Gunny taking a picture of her.

Mariana felt her cheeks warm even now, in the shower. After listening to Shane and Duke tell her stories about Jax and Jameson, she felt kind of guilty. Not like she intended to end up in a middle of a self-defense training session. She had a feeling Gia wanted her to learn a few moves. It must have had something to do with her past. Jax and Jameson mentioned how Gia had been attacked and defended herself.

Mariana was having a fun time the last few days. She had to admit, despite the little Shane incident, she was impressed at the dojo with Gia and Sensei Lee. She met Duke and Shane, who initially hit on her until finding out from Gia that she was taken. Then of course the guys told her stories about Jameson and Jax that had her rolling with laughter.

Then they mentioned the friends that were lost during their time in the Marines and about how Jameson and Jax saved a lot of fellow soldiers' lives.

"You should hear the way the men still talk about Jax and Jameson. Those guys talk about how they thought their lives were over. A group of seven men, all injured, all caught in the middle of a fierce fight on the ground in Afghanistan," Duke had begun to say and then shook his head and closed his eyes as if he remembered the other soldiers' recollection of events so vividly himself.

Then Shane continued telling the story.

"Jax and Jameson came out of nowhere. The guys said all they could see was smoke, and all they could hear were rounds and rounds of gunfire, when Jameson and Jax emerged from the smoke like two angels to the rescue. Those two men are brave. They're special." She had felt the tears in her eyes right then, just as she felt now, recalling the emotion Shane and Duke expressed.

Then of course they started telling her she should be with Shane and Duke.

Mariana shook her head. They didn't mean it. She figured at the time they were trying to cover up how emotional they had been getting over talking about the war and their experience. They were both very attractive men, but she only had eyes for Jax and Jameson.

She continued to lather the soap up on the washcloth as she inhaled the clean scent.

The best part about the last few days was that she felt relaxed and comfortable. Even after an excruciating workout by Sensei Lee. The man was a beast of an instructor. She did learn a lot of moves in self-defense. She also asked that Gia not let Jameson and Jax know that Duke and Shane were her partners when learning. Of course today, after the training session, Gunner stopped in to see Gia. Mariana was in an odd position under Shane. She had her legs wrapped around his ribs and her arms wrapped around his neck. Sensei Lee was trying to teach her how to tire out an attacker who had her on the ground in such a position. As she looked up, Gunny was snapping a picture with his camera. Gia had yelled at him to stop. Mariana shook her head. That stinker knew exactly what he was doing. Gunner was going to try and stir Jax and Jameson up. She didn't need that.

Jax and Jameson had seemed quite jealous of other men. It was like they were insecure about the relationship. That made her feel less concerned over her insecure feelings. This was new to all three of them. The only thing hanging over her head now was the talk about pregnancy. She could already be pregnant.

She laid her hand over her belly then rinsed the soap off her body as the shower water cascaded over her. She had a funny feeling in her gut. It was a combination of nerves and her insecurities. She decided to analyze the situation as she saw it. Worst-case scenario was that Jax and Jameson wouldn't want children and that they would be angry at her for getting pregnant. If that happened, she could probably go back to working for Freda until she started to show in her belly. No man would want a pregnant woman escorting them around Houston. They wanted sexy, beautiful, and smart women. God, this was looking worse than better. She couldn't ride the skateboard and be a courier. Plus, once the baby came, she would have to find other means of financial support. She felt the tears reach her eyes. She was in love with Jax and Jameson. She would die if they didn't want her and the baby. *What are you thinking? You don't even know if you're pregnant.*

She turned off the water and started drying off when she heard someone calling her name. Jax and Jameson were home from wherever it was they disappeared to this morning. The last few days had been filled with activities. She looked forward to snuggling on the couch with them.

"Mariana!"

"I'm in here," she called out and was a bit shocked when Jax shoved open the door and glared at her. Jameson looked none the happier.

"What in the hell were you doing in the fucking dojo with Shane?" Jax raised his voice.

Oh damn, Gunner sent him the picture. What a troublemaker.

"First of all, stop yelling."

"Stop yelling? I should toss you over my knee and spank your ass for allowing another man to touch you, never mind lay on top of you."

Spank me? Is he serious?

"Don't look at me like that."

"He'll do it. We both will," Jameson added, and she suddenly felt very aroused at their idea of punishment. Was she insane?

She placed her hands on her hips and nearly lost the towel that was wrapped around her body. She attempted again to look annoyed and place her hands on her hips, but the damn towel wouldn't stay in place.

"I have never been spanked in my entire life. You two have no such right to even think about doing such a thing."

"You think we don't?" Jameson asked, and Jax raised his hand up for Jameson to go no further.

"This. This is not acceptable." Jax held the phone out to her and she saw the picture. Yeah, it looked bad. She was underneath Shane, the giant of a man, and all she could see in the picture were her legs and her arms. Shane was smiling.

"I knew Gunner was up to something. That stinker took the picture when we weren't looking."

Jax raised his eyebrows at her.

"Oh, so you were sneaking around, lying underneath another man? Get your ass in the bedroom now."

She placed her hands on her hips and raised her voice.

"You are not going to spank me. No way, no how. I did nothing wrong." As she began to walk, the towel fell from her body, and Jax lifted her up into his arms.

Her breasts were level with his mouth as he squeezed her underneath her ass cheeks. Mariana held on to his shoulders as she stared down into his eyes.

"Jax, don't you dare do something you'll regret."

"I think you need to learn the rules of this relationship." He stomped toward the bed and sat down. She straddled his waist and tried to wiggle free. No such luck.

"Rules?" she asked.

"Yes," Jameson said as he began to undress.

"You belong to us. That means no other man ever touches you and definitely doesn't roll around on the floor with you."

"It wasn't like that. Sensei Lee was teaching me an escape move."

"It didn't look like you were trying to escape," Jax said through clenched teeth.

"I swear, it was nothing. Gunner was trying to rile you up with that picture."

"He sure as hell did that," Jameson said then pulled the belt from his pants and snapped the leather across the palm of his hand. She should be very frightened right now, but watching Jameson strike his hand with the thin strap of leather as he stared at her turned her on. She hoped that he wasn't going to spank her with that thing. *Oh God, I just creamed myself.*

"You shouldn't have placed yourself in that position to begin with. You belong to us and you need to start taking us seriously," Jax said as he slid the palms of his hands up and down her lower back.

"I'm sorry," she whispered to him.

Jax held her gaze. "You ought to be." In a flash he lifted her up and over his knees. She hung over his rock-solid thighs while he held her in position. She felt tight and so fully aroused she was actually leaking with excitement. She never thought something like this would turn her on, but from the start, Jameson and Jax's dominant, bossy behavior affected her.

"This is a reminder that we're the only men that get to touch this body," Jax said.

Smack.

"Oh."

"You're our woman and this is our ass."

Smack.

She gasped from the slap to her ass cheeks and held on to Jax's calves tightly. She couldn't believe how hard and aroused her nipples were. She was embarrassed as Jax ran the palm of his hand softly across both cheeks then dipped a finger into her pussy.

"Somebody likes getting spanked."

"Great, now she'll piss us off all the time to get her punishment," Jameson whispered as he stepped closer. "Look at me," Jameson said, and she turned to look up at him.

He continued to stroke that leather belt across the palm of his hand.

"I've got some wild fantasies running through my head right now," he admitted then snapped the belt softly against his palm. She felt her pussy tighten as she pulled her thighs together.

"Open up," Jax whispered as he maneuvered his fingers and fist between her thighs. She felt two fingers insert into her pussy, and she opened her mouth and moaned softly. She still held Jameson's gaze.

"How can we make you understand that you're all ours? That we want to keep you forever?" Jax added, and the tears stung her eyes.

"Don't you want that?" Jameson asked then gently trailed the leather belt across her ass cheeks then between her shaking thighs.

"Don't you want us forever?" Jameson asked while moving the soft leather back and forth against her slit and between her ass cheeks.

"Oh," she moaned.

Snap.

He tapped the leather against her ass cheeks, and she jumped. She never felt so aroused and filled with lust. He was making her entire body shake. The anticipation of not knowing their next moves or when they would strike was killing her.

Snap.

He did it again, and she moaned and thrust backward against Jax's finger strokes.

"Damn, baby, you look so fucking hot like this," Jax said then pumped his fingers a little faster into her cunt.

She gripped his legs and began to move against his thrusts. Jameson snapped the belt again against her ass cheeks, and she felt the tiny spasms of cream release again.

"Oh God, I can't take it. Please do something."

Jax lifted her up and turned her to the side as he placed her on the bed. Jameson threw down the belt and spread her legs wide. He was naked in front of her as Jax began to divest himself of his clothing.

Jameson looked so fierce and wild. His cock was huge and long, and she wanted him so badly that her pussy felt swollen with need.

"I can't stand to think of you with anyone else."

She shook her head.

"No one else. Just you and Jax," she said as Jameson thrust into her in one full stroke.

She gasped as he pulled back out then thrust forward again.

"Arms up," he told her, and she raised them back against the comforter.

"You're ours, Mariana. Always ours." He thrust again and again.

His much larger body covered hers as he continued to make love to her like a man on a mission. She wrapped her legs around his waist and counterthrust against him. He ran his hands along her hips to her breasts and pulled on her nipple hard. She screamed and thrust upward, trying to challenge his control. As she reached for his shoulders, he commanded for them to remain up.

"Keep them up there." He growled then grabbed for her wrists and held them down against the comforter as he stroked her cunt in hard, fast thrusts. His teeth were clenched, his neck muscles strained as he tried to claim her as deeply as he could. She felt his need, his desire as her breasts pushed upward and she screamed her release.

"Fuck, Mariana, you're mine. You belong to us." He thrust four more times very hard and very fast until he exploded inside of her. He continued to slowly rock his hips as he lay over her, kissing her breasts then her neck and shoulder until they calmed their breathing.

She closed her eyes and tried to relax until she felt Jameson move off of her. He still looked serious but a bit more content than earlier. Jax, on the other hand, looked fierce.

"Turn around on all fours," he ordered, and she once again felt her body react to his dominant commands. But this time, she felt a bit more cocky and sexy as she slowly turned over and provocatively got into position.

Smack

"Ouch."

"Mine," Jax said and grabbed her hips, pulled her back toward him, and the edge of the bed. She swallowed hard as he leaned over her.

"You want to learn the hard way, then you'll learn the hard way."

Oh shit, he's so damn sexy.

Her pussy wept, and just in the nick of time as Jax shoved into her pussy from behind.

* * * *

Jax felt nearly out of control and ready to explode. When he received that text message and picture from Gunner, he knew it was meant to piss him off. Shane was a dead man, too, for pulling this shit on them. Jax and Jameson were in love with Mariana, and their friends knew it. This was a means to a play to get under Jax's and Jameson's skin. However, their woman still needed to know that they had rules she needed to abide by. Rule number one was she belonged to them now, and no other man had a right to touch her. Lesson learned.

He absorbed the feel of being inside of her. The way she got so aroused with her first spanking and then how wet she got when Jameson added the belt. She was a true submissive, and he and Jameson were going to enjoy trying some fun and kinky shit with her in bed.

He stroked her tight little cunt over and over again. The sound of her moans and the way she pushed her ass back in counterthrusts was enough to do him in. He never wanted to claim anything or anyone more as his own except Mariana.

"This pussy, this ass is ours. This body belongs to us. If I ever get a picture of you with another guy again, never mind one on top of you, I'll kill him and then I'll deal with you."

He wrapped his arm around Mariana's waist as she exploded from his words. She was totally turned on by their dominance, and so were they. In and out, he stroked her pussy, trying to lessen the need to claim and win her. She was more than a possession, than a means to satisfy him sexually. Mariana had become everything in the world to him and Jameson, and their lives together had only just begun.

"Harder, Jax. Harder!" She raised her voice.

"Yes, ma'am."

He held her tight and rocked his body against hers. His goal was to reach her womb, a womb that someday would hold his and Jameson's child. She was all theirs for the taking.

"Forever, baby. Forever," he said through clenched teeth then thrust very fast and very hard into her. She moaned and screamed her release, and he followed suit as he climaxed and nearly fell against her in satisfaction.

* * * *

They lay together, the three of them on the bed. Jax caressed her inner thigh, and Jameson held her back against his chest as he caressed her breasts. She lay there completely naked and accepting of their love.

"You're amazing, baby," Jameson whispered.

"I love you both," she said in return, and they both smiled.

Jax trailed a finger over her pussy then back between her thighs.

"I love your body. One day, you'll be pregnant with our child, baby, and we'll be a family."

Mariana gasped and immediately tightened up.

"What did you say?"

Both men chuckled.

"Come on now, Sparks, you know we haven't used any protection for over a week. There's nothing to be scared about. We love you and we want you in our lives forever," Jameson said.

"But a baby? We hardly know one another."

"Mariana, we know one another very well. I'm sure that you're the one for me and for Jameson. I'm not letting you leave us, not ever."

He ran his palm across her belly, and she grabbed it, covering it with her own. Her heart soared at his words. She had been so worried that they would hate her or not want a baby with her.

The tear rolled down her cheek.

"Mariana, what's wrong?" Jax asked, and now Jameson sat up so that he could look at her, too.

"I was so scared. I was afraid that you wouldn't want a baby with me and that I would be a single mom. I worried about finding a job and not being able to support a baby on my own."

"Sweetheart, you're never going to be alone. You have us and we love you and when you get pregnant it is going to be the happiest moment of our lives, aside from the moment we met and fell in love with you," Jameson said, and she burst into tears as she hugged them both. They of course chuckled.

Chapter 14

Mariana woke up early the following morning, made herself a cup of coffee, and grabbed a big fleece blanket before she headed onto the porch. It was a cold winter morning, around forty degrees, but there was a slight breeze that made it feel colder. She cuddled under the blanket and sat on the large swinging bench and stared out at the open land.

She felt at peace for the first time in many years. She had eyed this bench and this porch the moment she arrived and knew that she would have to take the opportunity to enjoy it. A little bit of wintery cold weather wouldn't stop her. The only thing that had changed about that original thought was that her stay here with Jameson and Jax would be temporary. But last night, last night changed everything between them. She still didn't know if she was pregnant or not, but she knew that they loved her. She loved them, too, and actually she felt like this place, their home here could be hers, too.

She heard the door squeak open. "Damn, baby, what are you doing out here all alone in the cold?" Jameson asked as he pulled his jacket tighter. He was fully dressed in his sweats, sweatshirt, and jacket and probably headed to work out in the barn. They had a bunch of things set up in there, and she wondered why they didn't keep a gym inside of the house. She had asked Jax, and Jax told her that sometimes when they trained, they got a little wild and things got broken. She realized that they were both intense men and remained training like the commandos they once were in the military was a way of life. She liked that they did it. They had sexy, hot bodies because of it.

He joined her on the bench, and then the door opened again.

"You found her. Damn, I was worried," Jax stated as he ran a hand through his hair.

"What? Did you think I'd take off on you or something?" she teased. Jameson bumped his shoulder into hers and smiled.

"Don't get all sassy, you. I got a belt with your name on it." He raised his eyebrow and winked. She felt her cheeks warm and Jax placed his arm over her shoulder. They stared out toward the open land in front of them.

"This is so beautiful. It's quiet and all opened."

"You should see it in the spring and summer when the flowers are in bloom. There's a swimming pool out back and hot tub, too," Jax said.

"A swimming pool?" she asked, feeling very excited. Both men chuckled. She wondered if they found her youthfulness to be silly sometimes. It was a stupid thing to think about, but it did pop into her mind.

"What were you thinking about when you were out here all alone?" Jameson asked.

She was quiet a moment as she cuddled between them. Her body felt warm now. They had that instant effect on her.

"I was thinking that I really like it out here."

"I like it out here, too. I think of this house as more of a home than the penthouse," Jameson said.

"I don't know. I like being able to change things up a bit. It's like there's a separation of business life and personal life having both places," Jax added.

Jameson squeezed her hand and brought it up to his lips. He kissed the knuckles as he held her gaze. "This is a great place to raise a family."

She felt her heart race and her belly flutter. She smiled.

"Oh yeah, it will be wonderful to raise a family out here. The schools are really good, too," Jax added.

Mariana thought about that and about the life her unborn child or children might have. Especially with fathers like Jax and Jamison. Then came the feeling of fear gripping her insides.

"I know you two will make great fathers, but do you–do you think I'll make a good mommy someday?"

Jax sat forward. "Are you kidding me? You're going to be an awesome mom. You're so loving and caring and in tune to people. You'll be fantastic."

She smiled at his show of support and encouragement. This was what being parents was all about. They needed to communicate and talk things through.

She thought about her mother, and then suddenly she thought about Freda.

Mariana sat forward. Her jaw dropped as the tears hit her eyes.

"What's wrong?" Jameson asked. She looked at him and then at Jax.

"It's crazy, but the moment I thought about my mom, Freda popped into my head."

"Freda, really?" Jax asked.

"Sure she did. She loves you like a daughter already. I've never seen her so concerned over anyone ever," Jameson told her. That just validated her emotions.

"I like her a lot. I think she would love being part of my life, of our lives, especially if there is a baby involved. She can be like the grandmother," Mariana said then chuckled.

"I think she would love that," Jameson said.

"I think we should go to the drug store, get a test kit, and just find out if you're pregnant or not already. This is ridiculous," Jax said then stood up.

Mariana smiled.

"I was supposed to get my period yesterday. I'm game if you two are."

Jameson smiled.

"Let's get some breakfast and take the drive into town. We're only here a few more days until the art gala event at the community college that Rothesburgh is hosting," Jax said. They stood up and headed into the house. Mariana smiled as she covered her belly with her hand. She was pregnant, and she just knew she was.

* * * *

Mariana, Jax, and Jameson were back in Houston for the art exhibit. Mariana made plans to have lunch with Freda, so Jameson dropped her off at the estate. She was sitting in the dining room along with Freda, and they were talking about the house in the country and about Casper's.

"They are a great group of young men. They all had a difficult time serving in the military. I'm glad that you, Jax, and Jameson had time to spend together," Freda said then smiled.

Mariana felt so comfortable with Freda, she wanted the woman to be part of her celebration and her future.

"Freda, I'm moving in with Jax and Jameson and probably going to be living at the house in the country more often than the penthouse."

"That's wonderful news," Freda said but then seemed to be sad. Mariana reached over and covered her hand with her own. She held Freda's gaze and smiled.

"You've come to mean so much to me. As you know, I don't have a mother and never really had much of one. I was hoping that you would want to continue to be part of my life."

Freda gasped then used her free hand to cover her mouth as her eyes filled up with tears.

"Of course I want to be part of your life. I won't let those two dominating men keep us from getting together. You call me whenever you need to talk or you want to go shopping. We can do all the things that—"

"That a mother and daughter do?" Mariana completed her sentence, and they both smiled.

Freda covered Mariana's hand with both of hers.

"I would be honored."

Mariana stood up and so did Freda, and they hugged.

She pulled back and looked up into Freda's eyes.

"Freda, how do you feel about being a grandma?"

Freda gasped with her eyes wide open and then looked from Mariana's eyes to her belly then back to her eyes again.

"Are you?"

She nodded her head, and Freda cheered out loud then danced in a circle. Mariana laughed as Alvin came running into the room.

"Freda, is everything okay?"

"Yes, Alvin, everything is wonderful," she said as she grabbed Mariana's hands and squeezed them. She looked at Alvin who appeared utterly confused but smiled.

"Alvin, grab some champagne and some sparkling water for Mariana. I'm going to be a grandmother."

* * * *

Jameson was holding Mariana's hand and looking at a very provocative painting as Jax and Roldolpho discussed something that looked very serious.

Jameson spoke into the hidden mic on his sleeve to someone named Spider. The event was a complete success, and they were preparing to leave in just a little while.

"We're going to head out. I just wanted to say how wonderful it was to see you again, Mariana. You're simply glowing," Theo Centurion stated as he leaned forward and gave her a kiss on the cheek. He was escorted by a pretty blonde he had as an escort for the evening.

"It was nice seeing you again and thank you," Mariana replied. He stepped away from the blonde whom Jameson spoke to a moment while Theo whispered to Mariana.

"She can't compete with you or your love and knowledge of the arts. I wish Roldolpho had hired you for his gallery, but I guess since he sold it, that's out of the question. Good luck, dear, and see you soon."

Marian watched them walk away, and immediately Jameson was pulling her close.

"What did he whisper to you? I hope he wasn't making a pass."

"No, silly, he was complimenting my knowledge and love of the arts. He also said that Roldolpho sold the gallery. I can't believe it."

She felt kind of sad, but then, she wasn't serving hors d'oeuvres anymore, and come spring she would have her degree and look for a job for the time being.

"Hmm, that's interesting," Jameson said then looked back toward the painting.

"Do you mind if I use the ladies' room before we head out?"

"Of course not."

Just then Jax made that bird sound and Jameson immediately looked concerned.

"You can go see what's going on, I'll meet you up front, by the fountain?" she asked.

"Okay," he said then walked toward Jax. Mariana headed toward the ladies' room.

* * * *

"What's going on?"

"Where did Mariana go?" Jax asked, sounding concerned.

"The ladies' room."

"Let's get her out of here. Spider and the guys found some explosives in the back area of the displays."

"What? What kind of explosives? Why?"

"There are extra men around that don't normally work for Pro Tech securities. A large box truck, no plates, is parked down the street on the corner. Spider is interrogating some of the extra nonaccountable men. He also notified the owner of Pro Tech. He's furious and on his way here."

"Why the explosives?" Jameson asked as people started exiting the building. The exhibit technically ended thirty minutes ago.

"I don't know. Just go get Mariana and head out to the limo," Jax said, and as they turned around, an explosion rocked the whole entire first floor.

* * * *

Mariana grabbed onto the counter in the bathroom as a huge explosion seemed to rock the building. She immediately headed out of the ladies' room and saw the smoke encompass the area. Sirens were blaring, people were screaming and trying to exit the building, but the smoke grew thicker. It was so frightening, yet odd, that there was so much smoke. She debated about where to go.

To the left were smoke and a crowd of people trying to exit the door. To the right the same thing, but the smoke was encompassing the entire area. It was as if a huge smoke bomb went off.

Her heart was pounding inside of her chest. Instinctively she covered her hand over her belly and then thought about the panic button she had that night when Ellington attacked her. There was no button tonight. No need for an emergency panic button when two highly trained retired commandoes and security professionals flanked her side. *Oh God, Jameson and Jax? Please let them be okay.*

In a matter of seconds, she could hardly see but a few feet in front of her. There was so much smoke toward the front of the building and the exit. She didn't know what to do or where to head. As she turned to look behind her, she thought that she saw someone. A shadow through the thickness of smoke. Her throat began to tighten up and she started to cough.

"Come with me," a deep voice demanded then took her arm and dragged her right into the smoke. She pulled at his fingers that grasped her upper arm. "Let go of me." She coughed in between words, and then she noticed that he wore a mask. A gas mask?

"Let me go," she demanded then tried to drag her feet, but he didn't care. He just kept going into the thickness of the smoke. They reached a door, and she coughed some more as panic filled her body.

The door closed, and the smoke was lighter in this room.

He spoke into a mic. "I've got her. Bring the car around back. Move," he yelled at her then shoved her toward the door.

She didn't know who he was, but obviously he knew her and he wanted to take her out of here. Something was definitely wrong.

As the door opened, she heard the sirens down the block and saw the limo waiting there.

The man pulled off the gas mask, and she gasped. It was the man from the night Ellington attacked her. He met her at the bathroom and brought her to Ellington.

She turned around to open the back door, and he grabbed her around the waist and dragged her toward the car.

"Let me go. Leave me alone!" she screamed as he tossed her into the backseat just as the back door to the building slammed open.

She heard the bullets go off. The man jumped into the limo, and she tried to open the side door. He grabbed her legs, pulled her back, and as she turned he backhanded her across the mouth.

"Stupid bitch! You're nothing but trouble."

The car swerved as it took off in the opposite direction of the first responders.

* * * *

"What? Where is she?" Jax yelled into the sleeve of his jacket. Jameson was bent over next to him and coughing still. They had searched for Mariana and couldn't find her.

"Follow that damn limo!" Jax yelled then pulled Jameson up and walked him away from the crowd of police and firefighters.

"What's going on?" Jameson asked, standing up, finally taking a deep breath.

"Someone just threw Mariana into a limo."

"What?"

"Let's move."

They ran toward the unmarked police cruiser, and one of their employees, Brendan, was talking to the driver. He waved them over.

"The limo is en route to the airport. It belongs to Clover Masters. So does the box truck filled with stolen art from the event tonight. He planned to steal it all. We've got men on it and Rangers, too," Brendan stated.

"Let's get into the car and head after that limo. I'm going to kill Clover if he hurts Mariana," Jax said as they got into the unmarked car and the detective behind the wheel took off.

* * * *

"Let go of me," Mariana stated through clenched teeth as the thug held her arms behind her back. He had her kneeling on the floor as he spoke into his cell phone.

"I have her. We'll be there in five minutes."

By the time the car stopped, her face was really throbbing in pain. She was going to have a swollen and bruised cheekbone. She didn't know who was responsible for this situation, but she wasn't going to go willingly with this man. For all she knew it could be Ellington James who was the mastermind behind this.

As the car stopped she lost her balance and he let her go. She fell to the floor of the limo, and when she tried to get up, he went to grab her and she swung at his face. She must have hit him just right, because his head shot backward, almost like some cartoon character as it appeared like his head hit his shoulders then sprung forward. He grabbed his face and nose with both hands.

"You brokeded my nose," he said in a strange voice.

Brokeded?

Mariana crawled to the door, opened it, and fell out. It was dark outside as she tried to get her bearings, and then she heard his voice.

"Ahh, you've arrived right on schedule." Some other guy grabbed her by her hair and pulled her up from the ground. She had seen him before. As soon as he turned her toward the second car, a dark BMW, the door opened and a man stepped out.

Clover Masters?

She gasped then tried to pry the hands off of her hair.

"Let me go. What do you want?" she yelled.

"You're coming with me," Clover said then smiled. He looked her body over and licked his lips. "Get her into the car, Buster. The decoy worked. The art is on its way and the cops are none the wiser."

"You stole art from Darian?" she asked as she continued to struggle to get free. Buster was dragging her toward the BMW.

"I'm filthy rich now and you're my grand prize." Buster shoved her closer to Clover. Clover grabbed her face. "Looks like you didn't come willingly." He stared at her bruised cheekbone then leaned forward and kissed her on the mouth. She turned away, and Buster held her neck and head so that she was forced to stare into Clover's eyes.

"I wish I could see Jameson's and Jax's faces when they find out I've taken you away from them. I never did like those two assholes."

He placed his hand on her hip and then moved the palm of his hand up along her ribs to her breast.

"I'm going to enjoy having you."

Mariana was furious to think that this jerk thought he could take her. The fact that spoke with revenge against Jameson and Jax really pissed her off. So when he cupped her breast and Buster loosened his hold on her hair, she made her move.

"In your dreams, shithead," she exclaimed then rammed her knee up hard into his manhood. A quick back elbow to Buster's gut and then a twist of her body and she shoved him out of her way. *Thank you, Sensei Lee and Gia.*

She started to run. She wasn't sure which direction to go, but as sirens wailed in the background, she turned to look just as Buster tackled her to the ground.

Screaming, terrified that he might kill her, she instantly remembered the techniques she learned from Gia. A forearm to Buster's neck, a kick with her heels into his calf, the man yelled at her. He tried to straddle her body. She wrapped her legs around his ribs and squeezed as hard as he could. Around them, she could hear tires squeal. The BMW was blocked in, and she kept trying to hit Buster.

"You stupid bitch! You're going to die." He grabbed her by her throat and she dug her nails into his wrists, but he was determined to end her life. She thought about Jax and Jameson and about the baby just beginning to grow inside of her. She was struggling to get free, crying as she kicked him and scratched at his eyes. She remembered the move that Gia taught her. The one she thought was sick and could never do. She tried to scream but nothing came out, the pressure of Buster's hands against her throat were impeding her ability to breathe. With one final attempt to survive, to live to see Jax and Jameson and their baby, she grabbed a hold of Buster's head and pressed her thumbs and nails into his eye sockets on both sides.

His hold loosened as she heard yelling, and then Jameson struck Buster in the side of his face. Buster released his hold on her throat as Jameson tumbled on top of Buster. She curled into the fetal position, coughing for breath, crying hysterically, and relieved that she was still alive.

"Oh God, baby, are you okay?" Jax asked as he immediately got down on the ground beside her. He caressed her hair away from her eyes as she tried to calm down. Her heart was racing, her belly ached, and she feared that something would happen to the baby.

"Jax," she said then reached for him. He pulled her into his arms and across his lap. He looked her over, caressed his palm across her belly, then locked gazes with her.

"I'm so sorry we left you." He softly ran a finger along her neck, and when she swallowed it hurt.

"No, it wasn't your fault." She coughed.

"Don't talk. He hurt you. God, we saw him strangling you."

"Is she okay?" Jameson fell on his knees beside her. She turned to look at him. His face was red, he was breathing heavy, and his fists were at his sides. She knew that he and Jax rescued her. She saw him tackle Buster, and by the expression on his face, he still appeared angry.

"Buster and Clover?" she began to ask, instantly worried about her and the baby as she covered her belly with her hand.

"Neither one will bother you ever again," Jameson said.

"You didn't kill them, did you, Jameson?" Jax asked.

He stared at Mariana, and she felt the tears roll down her cheeks. Jameson reached down and wiped the tears away. "No, but I'm sure they wish they were dead. They'll both be in the hospital for quite some time."

Epilogue

It was early spring. The men were all outside cooking on the grill and talking with friends. Eve and Freda were talking about the new art show and surprise artist that would be on display tomorrow at Roldolpho's gallery.

"Hey, how come Jax didn't change the name of the art gallery still? I thought after he purchased it and then hired you as director, he was going to change it?" Eve asked. Mariana smiled then looked out the window at Roldolpho standing around a bunch of heterosexual men. He had his eye on Shane, and Shane was shaking his head in exasperation at Roldolpho's advances.

"Roldolpho means so much to us. We thought it should remain the name since he established the gallery years ago."

Gia and Mariana stood side by side as they sipped from their glasses of sweet tea. Mariana had been shocked to find out that Jax bought the gallery from Roldolpho and even more surprised when he asked her to be the director. It was a dream come true.

"So, are you going to give us a hint about the surprise artist?" Eve asked with a wink.

"I can't say, but maybe Gia can give a hint or two?" she said as Jax and Jameson walked into the house along with Gunny.

Gunny wrapped his arms around Gia and placed his hand over her small belly. She was expecting their first baby two months after Mariana's was due. Mariana was thrilled to share this experience with her new best friend, and so was Gia.

"What's going on?" Jax asked, giving Mariana a kiss on the cheek."

"We're trying to find out who the surprise artist is going to be tomorrow night," Freda said.

"Oh, the big secret. We don't know either. Mariana has kept the information under wraps."

"It will be worth the wait and the surprise, I promise," Mariana said, and then they started to bring the steaks and hot dogs into the house while the women placed homemade corn bread, salad, and roasted garlic potatoes onto the dining table.

Shane, Sensei Lee, Gunner, Garrett, Wes, John Luke, Jasper, Davie, and Eve all began to fill their plates. Jameson walked by and kissed Mariana softly on the lips before taking a plate, and Jax kept his hands on her shoulders as the others walked in and waited to fill their plates, too. She laughed at Roldolpho who followed Shane and Duke and spoke to them about fashion and posing in their underwear for a new male calendar he was working on. Both men looked livid. She chuckled as Jax released her and started talking to Teddy and Dale As Deanna walked into the room after baby Julia woke up from a nap.

This was Mariana's new family. Her baby would never be alone in the world again, and most importantly, her baby would always have a family that loved it.

"Hey, thanks for keeping my secret. If Gunny, Wes, and Garrett knew I was working so hard being pregnant, I'd never hear the end of it," Gia whispered.

Mariana smiled. "I think as soon as they find out that you're the secret artist about to be unveiled to the art world, they're going to be so proud of you. You're a beautiful artist and your paintings are going to be a huge hit. You'll see."

Gia gave Mariana a hug.

"I'm so glad that Jax and Jameson met you, fell in love, and knocked you up. Or I wouldn't have anyone to complain to, to boast to about my men, or enjoy being pregnant with."

Mariana felt the tears reach her eyes as she chuckled.

She ran her hand over her belly and looked at Jax and Jameson smiling and enjoying the time with family.

"Yeah, I guess I made out pretty good, getting 'knocked up' by two very sexy, extremely bossy but good-looking American soldiers, like Jax and Jameson."

Gia laughed. "Tell me about it," she said then picked up an empty plate.

Mariana couldn't help but thank the good Lord above for watching over her and leading her to Jax and Jameson. She was down and just trying to survive in hopes to achieve what were once impossible goals. She had learned that nothing was impossible with the love and support of her two men and of course of her newfound family.

To think that Jax and Jameson were once strangers, men of wealth whom she served hors d'oeuvres to and thought immediately how handsome they were. To then have them as lovers because their attraction was so strong that not even economic barriers or stigmas of rich and poor stood in the way. They simply saw her for whom she was, a young woman trying to make a better life for herself, one day at a time, one paycheck at a time while working two jobs and going to school.

Their instant attraction, love at first sight, brought them together, and now, because of that love a new family was growing and Mariana no longer saw life as a struggle to remain alive, but as a gift to make a difference in the world and to raise a family with the love, commitment, and encouragement she never had.

She looked at Jax and Jameson and their happy expressions. There was so much she wanted to tell them and to share with them as to how much they touched her and how important they were to her life. The words came in an instant today, in her mind and where her soul whispered what she couldn't say aloud.

I used to dream of love. I wanted to find it, but not waste time searching for it, when I was so determined to succeed in life. With my back against the obvious, it struck me like a bolt of lightning. There they were, two handsome men, standing in an art gallery, looking bored and unemotional. Then our eyes met. Double time, and I knew that something changed in me. Jax and Jameson Spaulding. You will always be my destiny, my lovers, my heroes, and my everything.

THE END

WWW.DIXIELYNNDWYER.COM

ABOUT THE AUTHOR

People seem to be more interested in my name than where I get my ideas for my stories from. So I might as well share the story behind my name with all my readers.

My momma was born and raised in New Orleans. At the age of twenty, she met and fell in love with an Irishman named Patrick Riley Dwyer. Needless to say, the family was a bit taken aback by this as they hoped she would marry a family friend. It was a modern day arranged marriage kind of thing and my momma downright refused.

Being that my momma's families were descendents of the original English speaking Southerners, they wanted the family blood line to stay pure. They were wealthy and my father's family was poor.

Despite attempts by my grandpapa to make Patrick leave and destroy the love between them, my parents married. They recently celebrated their sixtieth wedding anniversary.

I am one of six children born to Patrick and Lynn Dwyer. I am a combination of both Irish and a true Southern belle. With a name like Dixie Lynn Dwyer it's no wonder why people are curious about my name.

Just as my parents had a love story of their own, I grew up intrigued by the lifestyles of others. My imagination as well as my need to stray from the straight and narrow made me into the woman I am today.

For all titles by Dixie Lynn Dwyer, please visit
www.bookstrand.com/dixie-lynn-dwyer

Siren Publishing, Inc.
www.SirenPublishing.com

Lightning Source UK Ltd.
Milton Keynes UK
UKOW04f1054170813

215518UK00016B/1220/P